CAUSE TO FEAR

(AN AVERY BLACK MYSTERY—BOOK 4)

BLAKE PIERCE

Copyright © 2017 by Blake Pierce. All rights reserved. Except as permitted under the U.S. Copyright Act of 1976, no part of this publication may be reproduced, distributed or transmitted in any form or by any means, or stored in a database or retrieval system, without the prior permission of the author. This ebook is licensed for your personal enjoyment only. This ebook may not be re-sold or given away to other people. If you would like to share this book with another person, please purchase an additional copy for each recipient. If you're reading this book and did not purchase it, or it was not purchased for your use only, then please return it and purchase your own copy. Thank you for respecting the hard work of this author. This is a work of fiction. Names, characters, businesses, organizations, places, events, and incidents either are the product of the author's imagination or are used fictionally. Any resemblance to actual persons, living or dead, is entirely coincidental. Jacket image Copyright ozgurdonmaz, used under license from istock.com.
ISBN: 978-1-63291-949-6

BOOKS BY BLAKE PIERCE

RILEY PAIGE MYSTERY SERIES
ONCE GONE (Book #1)
ONCE TAKEN (Book #2)
ONCE CRAVED (Book #3)
ONCE LURED (Book #4)
ONCE HUNTED (Book #5)
ONCE PINED (Book #6)
ONCE FORSAKEN (Book #7)
ONCE COLD (Book #8)

MACKENZIE WHITE MYSTERY SERIES
BEFORE HE KILLS (Book #1)
BEFORE HE SEES (Book #2)
BEFORE HE COVETS (Book #3)
BEFORE HE TAKES (Book #4)
BEFORE HE NEEDS (Book #5)

AVERY BLACK MYSTERY SERIES
CAUSE TO KILL (Book #1)
CAUSE TO RUN (Book #2)
CAUSE TO HIDE (Book #3)
CAUSE TO FEAR (Book #4)

KERI LOCKE MYSTERY SERIES
A TRACE OF DEATH (Book #1)
A TRACE OF MURDER (Book #2)
A TRACE OF VICE (Book #3)

PROLOGUE

At thirty-nine years of age, Denice Napier could not remember a winter quite as cold as this one. While she had never really minded the cold, it was the bitter bite to the wind that unsettled her. She felt a gust sweep across the banks of the Charles River as she sat in a canvas chair, watching her kids skate, and she sucked in her breath. It was mid-January, and the temperature had barely broken double digits for the past week and a half.

Her kids, more clever than she cared to admit, had known that such drastic temperatures meant that most sections of the Charles River would be frozen over completely. That was why she had gone into the garage and dug out the ice skates for the first time this winter. She laced them up, sharpened the blades, and packed three thermoses of hot cocoa—one for her and one for each of her kids.

She watched them now, skating from bank to bank with the sort of reckless but beautiful speed only kids are capable of. The section they had come to, a straight but narrow section just through a strip of forest a mile and a half away from their home, was a complete sheet of ice. There was about twenty feet from bank to bank and then a wider expanse of about thirty feet or so that reached further out into the frigid river. Denice had clumsily gone onto the ice and set down little orange cones—the ones her kids sometimes used for soccer drills—to show them their borders.

She watched them now—Sam, nine years old, and Stacy, twelve—laughing together and actually enjoying each other's company. This was not something that happened very often so Denice was willing to put up with the bitter cold.

There were a few other kids out, too. Denice knew a few of them but not well enough to strike up a conversation with their parents, who were also sitting on the bank. Most of the other kids on the ice were older, probably in eighth or ninth grade from what Denice could tell. There were three boys playing a very disorganized game of hockey and another little girl practicing a spin move.

Denice checked her watch. She'd give her kids ten more minutes and then go home. Maybe they'd sit in front of the fireplace and watch something on Netflix. Maybe even one of those superhero movies that Sam was starting to like.

1

Her thoughts were interrupted by a piercing scream. She looked out onto the ice and saw that Stacy had fallen down. She was screaming, her face looking down toward the ice.

Every mother-based instinct raced through Denice in that moment. *Broken leg, twisted ankle, concussion...*

She'd gone through just about every possible scenario by the time she raced down to the ice. She skidded and slipped as she made her way to Stacy. Sam had also skated over to her and was looking down at the ice, too. Only, Sam wasn't screaming. He looked frozen, actually.

"Stacy?" Denice asked, barely able to hear herself over Stacy's screams. "Stacy, honey, what is it?"

"Mom?" Sam said. "What...what is it?"

Confused, Denice finally reached Stacy and dropped to her knees beside her. She looked to be unharmed. She stopped screaming once her mother was there with her but she was trembling now. She was also pointing to the ice and trying to open her mouth to say something.

"Stacy, what's the matter?"

Then Denice saw the shape under the ice.

It was a woman. Her face was a pale shade of blue and her eyes were opened wide. She stared up through the ice in a frozen state of terror. Blonde hair snaked this way and that from her skull, frozen in a position of disarray.

The face that stared back up at her, all wide eyes and pale skin, would revisit her in her nightmares for months to come.

But for now, all Denice could do was scream.

CHAPTER ONE

Avery could not remember the last time she'd shopped so recklessly. She wasn't sure how much money she had spent because she'd stopped paying attention after the second stop. Actually, she'd barely even looked at the receipts. Rose was with her and that, in and of itself, was priceless. She may feel differently about it when the bill came, but for now it was worth it.

With the evidence of her extravagance in little trendy shopping bags by her feet, Avery looked across the table to Rose. They were sitting in some trendy place in the Leather District of Boston, a place Rose had picked out called Caffe Nero. The coffee was outrageously priced but was the best Avery had tasted in quite a while.

Rose was on her phone, texting someone. Usually, this would anger Avery, but she was learning to let things go. If she and Rose were ever going to get their relationship right, there had to be some give and take. She had to remind herself that there were twenty-two years between them and that Rose was becoming a woman in a very different world than the one she had grown up in.

When Rose was done with her text, she set the phone down on the table and gave Avery an apologetic look.

"Sorry," she said.

"No need to be," Avery replied. "Can I ask who it is?"

Rose seemed to think about this for a moment. Avery was aware that Rose was also working on the give and take aspect of their relationship. She still had not decided how much of her personal life she wanted to let her mother into.

"Marcus," Rose said softly.

"Oh. I wasn't aware he was still a thing."

"He's not. Not really. Well…I don't know. Maybe he is."

Avery smiled at this, remembering what it was like when men were both confusing and intriguing all at once. "Well, are you dating?"

"I guess you could call it that," Rose said. She wasn't offering much in the way of words but Avery could see the red hues creeping into her daughter's cheeks.

"Does he treat you well?" Avery asked.

"Most of the time. We just want different things. He's not a very goal-oriented guy. Sort of directionless."

"Well, you know I don't mind hearing about things like this," Avery said. "I'm always willing to listen. Or talk. Or help you trash

3

guys that are hurting you. With my work…you're just about the only friend I have." She cringed internally at how cheesy it sounded but it was too late to take it back now.

"I know that, Mom," Rose said. Then, with a smirk, she added: "And I can't tell you how sad that sounds."

They shared a laugh at this but secretly, Avery was awed by how much Rose was like her in that moment. The instant any conversation became too emotional or personal, Rose tended to shut it down with either silence or humor. In other words, the apple hadn't fallen too far from the tree.

In the midst of their laughter, a dainty little waitress came over, the same one who had taken their orders and delivered their coffee. "Refills?" she asked.

"None for me," Avery said.

"Same here," Rose said. She then stood up as the waitress took her leave. "I actually need to get going," she said. "I've got that meeting with the academic advisor in an hour."

This was yet another thing Avery was afraid to make a big deal of. She was excited that Rose had finally decided to go to college. At nineteen, she'd made the moves and had set up appointments with advisors at a Boston-based community college. As far as Avery was concerned, that meant that she was ready to start making something of her life but was also not quite ready to leave familiar things—potentially including a strained yet fixable relationship with her mother.

"Call me later to know how it goes," Avery said.

"I will. Thanks again, Mom. This was surprisingly fun. We'll have to do it again sometime soon."

Avery gave a nod as she watched her daughter leave. She took the last gulp of her coffee and stood, gathering up the four shopping bags by her chair. After bundling them up around her shoulder, she left the coffee shop and headed for her car.

When her phone rang, it was quite an ordeal to answer it while carrying the shopping bags. She felt silly with the bags, actually. She had never been one of those women who liked to shop. But it had been a great mending exercise with Rose, and that was what was important.

After shifting all the bags around on her shoulder, she was finally able to reach the cell phone in her inner coat pocket.

"Avery Black," she said.

"Black," said the always-gruff and rapid voice of A1 Homicide Supervisor Dylan Connelly. "Where are you right now?"

"The Leather District," she said. "What's up?"

4

"I need you over at the Charles River, just outside of town over near Watertown, as fast as you can."

She heard the tone in his voice, the urgency, and her heart skipped a beat.

"What is it?" she said, almost afraid to ask.

There came a long pause, followed by a heavy sigh.

"We found a body under the ice," he said. "And you're going to have to see this one to believe it."

CHAPTER TWO

Avery arrived at the scene exactly twenty-seven minutes later. Watertown, Massachusetts, roughly twenty miles outside of Boston's city limits, was just one of the numerous towns that shared the Charles River with Boston. The Watertown Dam sat upstream of the Watertown Bridge. The area round the dam was mostly rural, as was the crime scene she was currently parking in front of. She estimated that the dam was still a good fifteen miles away, as the city of Watertown was another four miles up the road.

When she walked down to the river, Avery ducked under a long strip of crime scene tape. The crime scene was quite large, the yellow tape making a huge rectangle from two trees along the bank to two steel poles that the police had jammed into the solid ice on the river. Connelly was standing on the bank speaking with two other officers. Out on the ice, a team of three people were hunkered down on the ice, looking in.

She passed Connelly and gave him a wave. He glanced at his watch, gave an impressed look, and waved her on.

"Forensics can fill you in," he said.

That was fine with her. While she was growing to like Connelly more and more with each case, he was still best taken in small quantities. Avery made her way out onto the ice, wondering if those few times on a rink during her pre-teen years might serve her well. Apparently, though, those skills were long gone. She walked slowly, careful not to slip. She hated to feel vulnerable and not fully in control but the damned ice was just so slippery.

"It's okay," one of the Forensics members said, noticing her coming toward them. "Hatch fell on his ass three times getting out here."

"Shut up," said another member of the team, presumably Hatch.

Avery finally made it across to where the Forensics guys were huddled. They were hunched down, looking into a cleanly broken portion of ice. Beneath it, she saw the body of a nude woman. She looked to be in her early twenties. Pale and partially frozen skin aside, she looked quite striking. Gorgeous, actually.

Forensics had managed to hook the body beneath the arms with plastic poles. The end of each pole had a simple U-shaped bend to it, coated with what looked like some sort of cotton. To the right of the broken ice, a simple insulated blanket waited for the body.

"And she was found like this?" Avery asked.

6

"Yeah," said the man she assumed was named Hatch. "By kids, no less. The mom called the local PD and an hour and fifteen minutes later, here we are."

"You're Avery Black, right?" the third member asked.

"I am."

"You need to check things over before we take her out?"

"Yes, if you don't mind."

The three of them stepped back a bit. Hatch and the member who had called him out for busting his ass held on to the plastic poles. Avery inched closer; the toes of her shoes were less than six inches from the broken ice and open water.

The broken ice allowed her to see the woman from her brow all the way down to her knees. She looked almost like a wax figure. Avery knew the extreme temperatures might have something to do with that, but there was something else to her flawlessness. She was incredibly thin—maybe just a scrap over one hundred pounds. Her flushed face was turning a shade of blue but other than that, there were no blemishes—no scrapes, no cuts, no bruises or even pimples.

Avery also noticed that other than her soaked and partially frozen blonde hair, there was not a single hair on her body. Her legs were perfectly shaved, as was her pubic region. She looked like a life-sized doll.

With a final glance at the body, Avery stepped back. "I'm good," she told the Forensics team.

They came forward and with a count to three, pulled the body slowly from the water. When they pulled her out, they angled her so that she came out mostly on the insulated blanket. Avery noted that there was also a stretcher beneath the blanket.

With the body fully out of the water, she noticed two other things that struck her as odd. First, the woman was not wearing a single piece of jewelry. She knelt down and saw that her ears were pierced but there were no earrings. She then turned her attention to the second oddity: the woman's fingernails and toenails were neatly clipped—to the point of looking recently manicured.

It was odd, but this was what raised the most alarm bells in her mind. With the frigid flesh turning blue beneath those nails, there was something eerie about it. *It's almost like she's been polished,* she thought.

"We good here?" Hatch asked her.

She nodded.

As the three of them covered the body and then carefully trudged back toward the bank with the stretcher board, Avery

7

remained by the section of broken ice. She peered down into the water, thinking. She reached into her pocket, looking for a small piece of trash, but all she could find was a hair tie that had snapped on her earlier in the day.

"Black?" Connelly called from the bank. "What are you doing?"

She peered back and saw him standing close to the ice but being very purposeful to not step on it.

"Working," she hollered back. "Why don't you skate on out here and help?"

He rolled his eyes at her and she turned back to the ice. She dropped the snapped hair tie into the water and watched it bob up and down for a moment. Then it slowly caught the sluggish current of the water beneath the ice. It was pushed away and under the ice to her left, further out toward Watertown.

So she was dropped in somewhere else, Avery thought, looking down the river in the direction of Boston. On the bank, Connelly and the officer he had been speaking to were heading up behind the Forensics team.

Avery remained on the ice, standing straight up now. She was getting very cold as she watched her breath vaporize on the air. But something about the cold temperature seemed to center her. It allowed her to think, to use the light creaking noises of the ice as a metronome of sorts as she put her thoughts together.

Nude and not a blemish or bruise on her. So assault is ruled out. No jewelry, so it could have been a robbery. But most cases of a body after being robbed would show some signs of struggle...and this woman was spotless. And what about those nails and the absolute lack of hair anywhere other than her head?

She slowly walked to the bank, looking down the frozen river to where it rounded a bend and kept on in the direction of Boston. It was weird to think of how beautiful the frozen Charles River looked from Boston University while less than twenty minutes away a body had been pulled from it.

She pulled up her coat collar around her neck as she walked back to the bank. She was just in time to see the back doors of the Forensics van close. Connelly was approaching her but he was looking beyond her and out to the frozen water.

"You get a good look at her?" Avery asked.

"Yeah. She looked like a damn toy or something. All pale and cold and..."

"And perfect," Avery said. "Did you notice there was no hair on her? No bruises or bumps, either."

8

"Or jewelry," Connelly added. With a heavy sigh, he asked: "Dare I ask for your initial thoughts?"

She was much more willing to be unfiltered with Connelly now. She had been ever since he and O'Malley had offered her a promotion to sergeant two months ago. In return, they seemed more willing to accept her theories from the get-go rather than questioning the hell out of everything that came out of her mouth.

"Her fingernails were perfectly trimmed," she said. "It's like she had just come out of a salon before she was dumped in the river. Then there's the lack of hair anywhere. One of those things is odd enough but together, it screams intentionality to me."

"You think someone cleaned her up before they killed her?"

"Seems like it. It's almost like the funeral parlor making the dead look as presentable as possible for the open casket. Whoever did this cleaned her. Shaved her and did her nails."

"Any idea why?"

Avery shrugged. "I can only speculate right now. But I can tell you one thing that you probably aren't going to like very much."

"Ah hell," he said, knowing what was coming.

"This guy took his time...not even in the killing, but in how the body would look when it was found. He was intentional. Patient. Based on similar cases, I can almost guarantee you she won't be the only one."

With another of his patented sighs, Connelly dug his phone out of his pocket. "I'll call a meeting at the A1," he said. "I'll let them know we have a potential serial killer."

CHAPTER THREE

Avery supposed that if she was going to take the position of sergeant, she needed to get over her hatred of the A1 conference room. She had nothing against the room per se. But she knew that a meeting held within it so soon after the discovery of a body meant that there would be cross-talking and arguing, most of which would be used to shoot down her theories.

Maybe as sergeant, that will come to an end, she thought as she walked into the room.

Connelly was at the head of the table, shoving papers around. She figured O'Malley would be in soon. He'd seemed a lot more present at any meeting she was a part of ever since they had offered her the sergeant position.

Connelly looked up at her through the growing crowd of other officers. "Things are moving quickly on this one," he said. "The body pulled from the river was ID'ed exactly five minutes ago. Patty Dearborne, twenty-two years of age. A Boston University student and Boston native. Right now, that's all we know. The parents will need to be informed once this meeting is over."

He slid over a folder that contained only two sheets of paper. One showed a picture taken from Patty Dearborne's Facebook profile. The other sheet showed three photos, all taken from the Charles River earlier in the day. Patty Dearborne's face was present in all of them, her purple-tinted eyelids closed.

In a morbid train of thought, Avery tried to see the young woman's face in the same way a killer might see it. Patty was gorgeous, even in death. She had a body that Avery herself would have seen as far too skinny but bar-wandering men would salivate over. She used this mentality, trying to gauge why a killer would choose such a victim if there were no sexual implications.

Maybe he's after beautiful things. The question, of course, is if he is seeking these beautiful things in order to fawn over them or to destroy them. Does he appreciate beauty or does he want to obliterate it?

She wasn't sure how long she had been thinking about this. All she knew was that she jumped a bit when Connelly called the meeting to order. There were a total of nine people in the conference room. She saw that Ramirez had snuck in. He was in a seat near Connelly, looking through the same type of folder Connelly had given her moments ago. He apparently felt her looking at him; he glanced up and smiled at her.

She returned the smile as Connelly started. She dropped her gaze right away, not wanting to be too obvious. While just about everyone in the precinct knew that she and Ramirez were an item now, they still liked to try to keep it under wraps.

"Everyone should have been briefed by now," Connelly said. "For those of you that have not, the woman has been identified as Patty Dearborne, a BU senior. She was found in the Charles River just outside of Watertown but she is a Boston native. As Detective Black pointed out in the briefing you all received, the current of the river suggests that the body was dumped elsewhere. Forensics is guessing that her body was in the water for as long as twenty-four hours. Those two things add up to a probable dumping spot somewhere within Boston."

"Sir," Officer Finley spoke up. "Forgive me for asking, but why are we not even thinking about suicide? The briefing states there were no bruises and no signs of a struggle."

"I ruled that out almost right away when I saw that the victim was nude," Avery said. "While suicide would usually be something to consider, it's highly unlikely that Patty Dearborne stripped naked before jumping into the Charles River."

She almost hated to shoot Finley's ideas down. She was watching him become a damn good officer week by week. He'd matured over the last year or so, morphing out of the frat-boy persona most people knew him by and into a hard-working officer.

"But no bruises," another officer said. "That seems to be a smoking gun."

"Or evidence that it was *not* suicide," Avery argued. "If she jumped from any sort of height more than eight to ten feet, there would have been visible bruising on her body from the sheer impact."

"Forensics agrees with this," Connelly said. "They're going to be sending a more finalized report soon, but they feel pretty certain about this." He then looked to Avery and gestured to the table with a sweeping of his hand. "What else do you have, Detective Black?"

She took a moment to discuss the things she had pointed out to Connelly—details that were in the briefing. She mentioned the trimmed and polished nails, the lack of hair, and the absence of jewelry. "Another thing to point out," she added, "is that a killer that would go to these lengths to make his victims presentable suggests either a skewed admiration for the victim or some sort of regret."

"Regret?" Ramirez asked.

"Yes. He dolled her up and made her as beautiful as possible because maybe he didn't *mean* to kill her."

"Right down to shaving her...nether regions?" Finley asked.

"Yes."

"And tell them why you think we're dealing with a serial here, Black," Connelly said.

"Because even it if *was* a mistake, the fact that the killer did her nails and shaved her denotes patience. And when you add that to the fact that this woman was quite pretty and free of blemishes, it makes me think he's drawn to beauty."

"He has a funny way of showing it," someone else spoke up.

"Which leads me back to the line of thought that maybe he didn't mean to kill her."

"So you think it was like a date gone bad?" Finley asked.

"We can't be sure yet," she said. "But my first reaction is no. If he was this deliberate and careful with the way she looked before dumping the body, I think he likely put that same kind of care into selecting her."

"Selecting her for what, Black?" Connelly asked.

"I think that's what we need to find out. Hopefully Forensics will have some answers to lead us down the right path."

"So what do we do until then?" Finley asked.

"We bust our asses," Avery said. "We dig as deep into Patty Dearborne's life as we can, hoping to find some clue that will help us find this guy before he does it again."

When the meeting ended, Avery headed across the conference room to have a word with Ramirez. Someone needed to inform the parents of Patty Dearborne and she felt the need to do it. Speaking to grief-stricken parents, while incredibly difficult and emotionally draining, was usually one of the best places to find a lead right off the bat. She wanted Ramirez with her, wanting to keep working on the balance between their personal and professional lives. It was still tricky, but they were slowly getting the hang of it.

Before she made it to him, though, O'Malley came into the room. He was speaking on the phone, clearly in a hurry. Whatever he was dealing with, it must have been pressing for him to have missed the meeting about the Patty Dearborne case. He stood by the door, waited until everyone except Avery, Ramirez, and Connelly were gone, and then closed the door. He ended his call with a quick and almost rude *"Yeah, later,"* and then took a deep breath.

"Sorry I missed the meeting," he said. "Anything big come up?"

"No," Connelly said. "We've got the woman ID'ed and now need to tell her family. We're working on the assumption that whoever did this will do it again."

"Black, can you send me a quick report explaining the details?" O'Malley asked.

"Yes sir," she said. He never asked her for small things like that. She wondered if it was another of his not-so-subtle tests. She'd noticed him being more lenient with her over the last few weeks, more willing to give her more responsibility without interference. She was sure it all had to do with them asking her to take sergeant.

"While both of you are here," O'Malley said, looking at Avery and Ramirez, "I'd like to have a word. A few words, actually…and I don't have a lot of time, so I'll make it quick. First…I'm totally fine with the two of you seeing one another outside of work. I thought long and hard about breaking you up here at the A1 but damn it…you work too well together. So as long as you two can tolerate the in-jokes and speculations, you're going to remain partners. That good?"

"Yes sir," Ramirez said. Avery nodded in agreement.

"The next thing…Black. The whole sergeant thing…I'm going to need a decision soon. As in, within forty-eight hours. I've tried to be patient, letting you work things out. But it's been over two months now. I think that's fair."

"It *is* fair," she said. "I'll let you know something by tomorrow."

Ramirez gave her a look of surprise. Truth be told, her response had surprised *her*, too. Deep down, though, she thought she knew what she wanted.

"Now, on this lady-in-the-river case," O'Malley said. "It's officially yours, Black. Take Ramirez with you, but let's keep it professional."

Avery was a bit embarrassed that she found herself blushing. *Ah God,* she thought. *First a shopping spree and now blushing over a boy. What the hell has happened to me?*

To keep things rolling and not get thrown off of her game, Avery turned things directly back to the case. "I'd like to be the one to notify the family."

"We can delegate that to someone else," Connelly suggested.

"I know. But as terrible as it sounds, parents receiving such terrible news are usually the best resources for information. Everything is raw and open."

"My God, that's pretty heartless," Connelly said.

"But effective," O'Malley said. "Good deal, Black. It's four fifty right now. With any luck, you'll catch them getting off of work. I'll make sure someone texts you the address within the next ten minutes. Now get to it. Dismissed."

Avery and Ramirez took their leave. Out in the hall, the nine-to-fivers were starting wrap up their day. But for Avery, the day was far from over. In fact, with the task of breaking the news of a young woman's death to her parents on the horizon, Avery thought it was going to turn out to be one hell of a long night.

CHAPTER FOUR

The Dearbornes lived in a quaint little house in Somerville. Avery read over the information that had been texted and emailed to her while Ramirez drove. Patty Dearborne had been a great student, in her senior year at BU with intentions of becoming a counselor for a behavioral health firm. Her mother, Wendy, was a trauma nurse who rotated through two different area hospitals. Patty's father, Richard, was a business development manager for a large telecommunications company. They were a well-to-do family with not a single speck of dirt on their record.

And Avery was about to tell them that their daughter was dead. Not only dead, but that she had been dumped into a frigid river completely nude.

"So," Ramirez said as he wound through the rustic little streets of the Somerville neighborhoods. "Are you going to take the sergeant gig?"

"I don't know yet," she said.

"Any inkling?"

She pondered this for a moment and then shook her head. "I don't want to talk about that right now. It seems small in comparison to what we're about to do."

"Hey, you volunteered for this," he pointed out.

"I know," she said, still not certain why. Yes, her thoughts about getting a good lead were true, but she felt like there was something else. Patty Dearborne had only been three years older than Rose. It was far too easy to see Rose's face on that frozen body. For some bizarre reason, it made Avery feel that she needed to break the news to the family. Maybe it was a maternal-based urge, but she felt that she owed it to the parents in some strange way.

"So let me ask you this," he said. "What makes you so sure this isn't just a one-time thing? Maybe an ex-boyfriend just lost his shit. Maybe this is a one and done."

She grinned briefly because she knew he wasn't arguing with her. Not really. She had noticed that he liked to get glimpses into how her mind worked. His rebuttal of her theories was simply a way to get her primed up.

"Because based on what we know about the body, this guy was careful and meticulous. An enraged ex-boyfriend would not be so careful about not leaving bruises. The finger- and toenails are the clincher for me. Someone took their time with them. I'm hoping the

15

parents will be able to provide more insight into the sort of woman Patty was. If we know more about her, we'll know exactly how much of the primping was done by whoever dumped the body."

"Speaking of which," Ramirez said, pointing ahead. "Here we are. You ready for this?"

She took a deep, shaky breath. She loved her job but this was the one part she absolutely dreaded. "Yeah, let's go," she said.

Before Ramirez had time to say another word, Avery opened the door and stepped out.

She braced herself.

***

Avery knew that no two people responded to grief in the exact same way. That's why she was not all that surprised when, fifteen minutes later, Wendy Dearborne was nearly in a state of shock while Richard Dearborne was a loud and frantic mess. At one point, she feared he would become violent when he slapped at a vase on the kitchen table and sent it crashing to the floor.

The weight of the news hung heavy in the room. Avery and Ramirez had remained quiet, speaking only when asked a question. In the silence, Avery saw two pictures of Patty in the living room; one was on the mantel above the fireplace and another was a canvas hanging on the far living room wall. Avery's suspicion had been right. The girl had been absolutely stunning.

Wendy and Richard were both sitting on the couch in the living room now. Wendy had gotten slight control of herself, letting out the occasional gut-wrenching sob as she lay against Richard's shoulder.

With tears streaming down his face, Richard looked at Avery. "Can we see her? When can we see her?"

"Right now, Forensics is still trying to determine what might have happened to her. As you might imagine, the cold water and frigid temperatures make it harder to find clues or evidence. In the meantime, there are a few questions I'd like to ask you that may help us find answers."

Both of them wore looks of confusion and absolute horror on their faces but it was clear that Wendy would be no help. She was stunned into silence, taking the occasional look around the living room as if checking to make sure she knew where she was.

"Of course, whatever questions you have," Richard said. Avery thought the man was tough deep inside—perhaps trying to figure out some answers on his own.

"I know it's going to seem like a strange question," Avery said. "But was Patty the sort of girl to get really intricate with grooming and fingernails? Things like that?"

Richard let out a whimper and shook his head. He was still crying but was at least able to form words between his hitches for breath. "Not at all. She was actually sort of a tomboy. On any given day, I bet you'd find dirt under her nails before you found them with nail polish. She did get dolled up from time to time but only on special occasions. She sometimes paid a lot of attention to her hair, but she's not—she *wasn't*—a girl's girl, you know?"

Correcting himself on *wasn't* seemed to break something within Richard Dearborne. Avery hid her own little cringe as her heart broke for him. It was enough to make her decide not to ask the next question she had planned—a question about the frequency in which Patty shaved her legs. Avery thought it was a safe bet that if she was a tomboy who cared little for her nails, she probably wasn't obsessive about shaving her legs. There was no need to ask the question to a man who had just lost his daughter.

"Do you know of any enemies Patty had? Anyone she had a history of problems with?"

The question took a moment to sink in. When it finally did, the flicker of anger she had seen earlier returned to Richard Dearborne's eyes. He got up from the couch but was held in place by his wife's groping hand on his wrist.

"That motherfucker," Richard spat. "Yes. Oh yes, I can think of someone and I bet you *anything*...oh God..."

"Mr. Dearborne?" Ramirez asked. He had slowly gotten to his feet, perhaps anticipating some sort of rage-filled lashing out from Richard.

"Allen Haggerty. He was a high school boyfriend that just wouldn't let go when things eventually ended two years into college."

"Did he cause any problems?" Ramirez asked.

"Yeah. So much so that Patty had to get a restraining order placed against him. He was waiting outside of her classes for her. It got so bad that Patty lived here last year because she didn't feel safe at the dorms."

"Did he ever get violent?" Avery asked.

"If he did, Patty never said anything. I know he tried to touch her—hugs and kisses and things like that. But she never said anything about hitting her."

"The note..."

Wendy Dearborne's voice was so light that it was like wind. She would still not look at Avery or Ramirez. Her eyes were downcast, her mouth partially open.

"What note?" Avery asked.

"A note that Patty never showed us but we found in her pockets while doing laundry while she was living here," Richard said. "The creep left a note pinned to her dorm room door. She never said so, but we think it was the deciding factor in her moving back here. I don't remember it word for word but it talked about how he thought about killing himself because he could not have her but how it sometimes made him angry. Some dark stuff about how if he couldn't have her, no one could."

"Do you still have the note?" Avery asked.

"No. When we confronted Patty about it, she threw it away."

"How long did she stay here?" Avery asked.

"Until last summer," Richard answered. "She said she was tired of living in fear. We made the decision that if anything happened with Allen again, we'd directly get the police involved. And now...now *this*..."

A heavy silence blanketed the room, until finally he looked up at them. Avery could feel the father's grief and rage in that stare.

"I know it's him," he said.

CHAPTER FIVE

As Avery and Ramirez staked out the block surrounding Allen Haggerty's address, she received Haggerty's file via email. She was surprised to find little on it. He had three speeding tickets since the age of seventeen and had been briefly arrested at a mostly non-violent protest in New York City four years ago, but nothing serious.

Maybe he just went a little nuts when Patty tried leaving him, she thought. She knew it happened from time to time. It was, in fact, one of the most prominent excuses given by violent husbands who beat their wives. It came down to jealousy, a lack of control, and feeling vulnerable.

No one was home, so within an hour and a half of informing the Dearbornes that their daughter was dead, there was an APB out for him. While canvassing the neighborhood, Ramirez once again showed Avery just how in tune he was with her. "This whole thing is making you think of Rose, isn't it?" he asked.

"It is," she admitted. "How did you figure that out?"

He smiled. "Because I know your face very well. I know when you're pissed, I know when you're embarrassed, uneasy, and happy. I also noticed how you quickly looked away from the pictures of Patty in the Dearborne house. Patty wasn't much older than Rose. I get it. Is that why you insisted on breaking the news to her parents?"

"Yes. Good catch."

"It happens from time to time," he said.

It wasn't until 10:08 that Avery's phone rang. Connelly was on the line, sounding both tired and excited. "We've located Allen Haggerty coming out of a bar in the Leather District," he said. "We've got two of our guys holding him for you. How soon can you be there?"

The Leather District, she thought. *That's where Rose and I were earlier today, thinking how good our lives were and how timidly we were repairing our relationship. And now there's a potential killer in that same location. It feels...weird. Like coming full circle in some strange way.*

"Black?"

"Ten minutes," she answered. "What's the bar?"

She took down the information and just like that, Ramirez drove them into the very same area of the city where she had, less than twelve hours ago, been enjoying time with her daughter.

19

Knowing that was something that Wendy Dearborne would never again get to do sat heavy on her heart. It also made her a little angry.

Quite frankly, she couldn't wait to grill this little sonofabitch.

***

The two officers who had located Allen Haggerty seemed happy to hand him off. One of the officers was a guy Avery had gotten to know fairly well—an older man who would likely be retiring within a few years. His name was Andy Liu and he always seemed to have a smile on his face. But not now. Now, he seemed irritated.

The four of them met outside of Andy Liu's patrol car. In the back seat, Allen Haggerty peered out at them, confused and clearly pissed off. A few people passing by to bar-hop on a Friday night tried to see what was going on without being too obvious.

"He give you any problems?" Ramirez asked.

"Not really," Andy's partner said. "He's just a little drunk. We were almost ready to take him to the precinct and give him a nice interrogation room, but O'Malley said he wanted you to talk to him before we made that sort of decision."

"Does he know why you want to speak with him?" Avery asked.

"We told him about Patty Dearborne's death," Andy said. "That's when he really lost his mind. I tried to keep it civil in the bar but in the end, I had to cuff him."

"That's fine," Avery said. She looked into the back of the patrol car and frowned. "Do you mind if we borrow your car for a second?"

"Help yourself," Andy said.

Avery took the driver's side while Ramirez slid into the passenger seat. They angled themselves to the side to peer easily into the back at Allen.

"So how did it happen?" Allen asked. "How did she die?"

"That's still not clear," Avery said, not seeing any reason to be vague with him. She'd learned a long time ago that honesty was always the best approach if you wanted to get a proper read on a potential suspect. "Her body was discovered in a frozen river, under the ice. We don't have sufficient information to know if that was what killed her or if she was killed before being thrown into the river."

20

That might have been a little harsh, Avery thought as she watched a soft shock fill Allen's face. Still, seeing that genuine expression on his face was all she needed to have a good feeling that Allen Haggerty had nothing to do with Patty's death.

"When was the last time you saw her?" Avery asked.

It was clear that he was having to struggle to think about it. Avery was pretty sure that by the time the night was over, Allen would shed more than a few years over his now-deceased lost love.

"A little over a year ago, I guess," he finally answered. "And that was purely coincidental. I ran into her as she was coming out of a grocery store. We looked at each other for like two seconds and then she hurried off. And I don't blame her. I was an asshole to her. I got pretty obsessed."

"And there has been no contact since then?" Avery asked.

"None. I faced the facts. She was done with me. And being obsessed with someone really isn't the way to win them over, you know?"

"Do you know of anyone in her life that might be capable of doing something like this to her?" Ramirez asked.

Again, there was a struggle behind Allen's eyes as he tried to piece it all together. As he thought about this, Avery's phone rang. She glanced at the display and saw that it was O'Malley.

"Yeah?" she asked, answering quickly.

"Where are you?" he asked.

"Speaking with the ex-boyfriend."

"Any chance he might be the one we're looking for?"

"Highly doubtful," she said, continuing to watch the sorrow overtake Allen's face in the back seat.

"Good. I need you back at the station on the double."

"Is everything okay?" she asked.

"That depends on how you look at it," O'Malley replied. "We just got a letter from the killer."

21

CHAPTER SIX

Even before Avery and Ramirez were able to get into the precinct, Avery could tell that this situation had gotten out of hand. She had to carefully maneuver the car through the A1 parking lot to not hit reporters or clip news vans. The place was an absolute circus and they had not even gotten inside yet.

"This looks bad," Ramirez said.

"It does," she said. "How in the hell did the press find out about this letter if it came directly to the precinct?"

Ramirez could only shrug as they got out of the car and hurried inside. A few reporters got in the way, one of whom practically stepped out in front of Avery. She nearly collided with him but sidestepped him just in time. She heard him call her a bitch under his breath but that was the least of her concerns.

They fought their way to the door, with reporters clamoring for comment and flashbulbs going off. Avery felt her blood boiling and would have given anything in that moment to punch one of those nosy ass reporters directly in the nose.

When they finally made it into the precinct with the doors closed and locked securely behind them, she saw that the inside wasn't much better. She'd seen the A1 in a state of urgency and disarray before, but this was something new. *Maybe there's a leak in the A1,* Avery thought as she walked quickly toward Connelly's office. Before she reached it, though, she saw him storming down the hallway. O'Malley and Finley were marching behind him.

"Conference room," Connelly barked.

Avery nodded, taking a right a few feet further down the hall. She noticed that no one else was milling around the conference room door, meaning that this meeting was going to be small. And those types of meetings were typically not pleasant. She and Ramirez followed Connelly into the room. The moment O'Malley and Finley were also inside, Connelly shut the door and locked it.

He threw a sheet of paper down onto the conference room table. It was covered in a clear plastic sheet, causing it to slide almost perfectly in Avery's direction. She picked it up carefully and looked at it.

"Just read it," Connelly said. He was frustrated and looked a little pale. His hair was in disarray and there was a wild look in his eyes.

Avery did as instructed. Without removing the single sheet of paper, she read the letter. With each word she read, the room seemed to grow colder.

Ice is beautiful, but it kills. Think of the gorgeous sparkle of a thin layer of frost on your windshield on a late fall morning. That same pretty ice is killing plant life.

It's efficient in its beauty. And the flower comes back...always comes back. Rebirth.

The cold is erotic, but it maims. Think of being extremely cold coming out of a winter storm and then curling up naked with a lover under the sheets.

Are you chilled yet? Can you feel the iciness of being outsmarted?

There will be more. More cold bodies, floating into the afterlife.

I dare you to try to stop me.

You'll succumb to the cold before you find me. And while you're freezing, wondering what happened just like the flowers burdened with frost, I'll be long gone.

"When did this come in?" Avery asked, setting the letter back on the desk for Ramirez to read.

"Sometime today," Connelly said. "The envelope itself wasn't opened until about an hour ago."

"How in the hell did the press know already?" Ramirez asked.

"Because every local news network also received a copy of it."

"Holy shit," Ramirez said.

"Do we know when the media got their copies?" Avery asked.

"It was sent via email a little over an hour ago. We assume it's so it would get there in time to make the eleven o'clock news."

"Where was it emailed from?" Avery asked.

"Oh, this is the screwed up part...well, *one* screwed up part," O'Malley said. "The email address is registered to a woman named Mildred Spencer. She's a seventy-two-year-old widow that only has the email address to keep in touch with her grandkids. We've got someone talking to her right now, but all signs point to the account being hacked."

"Can we trace the hack?" Avery asked.

"No one at the A1 has the capabilities. We've called the State Police to try to crack it."

Ramirez was done with the letter, sliding it back to the center of the table. Avery slid it back over to her and eyed it again. She did not read it again, but just studied it: the paper, the handwriting, the odd placement of sentences on the paper.

"Any initial thoughts, Black?" Connelly asked.

"A few. First, where's the envelope it came in?"

"Back at my desk. Finley, run fetch it, would you?"

Finley did as he had been asked while Avery continued to pore over the letter. The handwriting was pristine but also sort of childlike. It looked like someone had gone to great lengths to perfect it. There were also a few key words that jumped out to her as being quite odd.

"What else?" Connelly asked.

"Well, a few things right off the bat. The fact that he sent us a letter makes it clear that he wants us to know it's him—without knowing his identity. So while it might not be a game to him per se, it's something he wants credit for. He also *enjoys* being hunted down. He *wants* us to go after him."

"Are there any clues in there?" O'Malley asked. "I've looked it over at least a dozen times and I'm getting nothing."

"Well, the wording is weird in some places. The mention of a windshield in a letter where the only other concrete thing he references are flowers and bed covers seems strange. I think it's also worth noting that he used the words *erotic* and *lover.* Pair that with the fact that the victim we found today was pretty much gorgeous and there's got to be something there. The mention of *afterlife* and *rebirth* is unsettling, too. But we could go a million different ways with that until we know more."

"Anything else?" Ramirez asked with his usual not-so-concealed smile. He loved to see her on a roll. She tried to push this to the back of her mind as she went on.

"The way he breaks his lines up…it's almost like fragmented stanzas of poetry. Most every other letter I've ever seen in old case studies where the killer contacted the police or media was usually in blocks of text."

"How's that a clue?" Connelly asked.

"It might not be," Avery said. "I'm just free-styling here."

A knock came at the door. Connelly opened it and Finley stepped back in. He closed the door behind him, setting the lock. He then carefully placed the envelope on the table. There was nothing remarkable about it. The address to the station had been written in the same carefully practiced script that was on the letter. There was no return address and a Forever stamp in the left corner. The postmark was high on the envelope and mostly to the left, its edges touching the stamp.

24

"It came from zip code 02199," O'Malley said. "But that means nothing. The killer could have gone miles outside of his area to mail it."

"That's true," Avery said. "And this guy seems too smart and determined to lead us right to him via a zip code. He'd have thought about that. The zip code is a dead end, I can guarantee it."

"So then what does that leave us to go on?" Finley asked.

"Well," Avery said, "this guy seems to be preoccupied with the cold, with ice in particular. And not just because that's where we found the body. It's all over the letter. He seems to be fixated on it. So I wonder…can we run a search for anything dealing with ice or the cold? Ice skating rinks, meat lockers, labs, anything."

"You're certain the location isn't purposeful?" Connelly asked. "If he wants to be known, maybe the zip code was like a calling card."

"No, I'm not certain. Not at all. But if we can find a business or some other organization that deals in ice or just the cold inside of that zip code, I'd maybe start there."

"Okay," Finley said. "So do we need to check security tapes around the locations of post offices or drop boxes?"

"God no," Connelly said. "It'll take forever and there's no way we'd know when this particular letter was sent."

"We need a list of those businesses and organizations," Avery said. "That's going to be the best place to start. Can anyone think of any right off the top of their heads?"

After several moments of silence, Connelly let out a sigh. "I don't know right off the top of my head," he said. "But I can have you a list within half an hour. Finley, can you get that request rolling?"

"On it," Finley said.

When he was out of the room again, Avery raised an eyebrow in Connelly's direction. "Is Finley an errand boy now?"

"Not at all. You're not the only one up for a promotion. I'm trying to get him more involved in every aspect of high-profile cases. And as you know, he thinks you walk on water so I'm giving him a chance on this one."

"And why are we locking ourselves in the conference room?" she asked.

"Because the press is on this. I don't want to take any chances with bugged rooms or tapped phone lines."

"Seems paranoid," Ramirez said.

"Seems *smart*," Connelly said with a bit of venom.

25

Wanting to prevent a pissing match between the two, Avery pulled the letter closer to her. "You mind if I eyeball this letter some more while we wait on results?"

"Please do. I'd much rather have someone on the A1 figure it out before the media blasts it all over TV and some nerdy kid in a basement figures it out."

"We need to get Forensics on this. A handwriting analysis should be done. The envelope needs to be looked over for any trace evidence: fingerprints, dust filaments, anything."

"They've been notified and the letter is going to them right away the moment you're done with it."

"It's got to be done quickly," she said. "I know you were just making a joke about some kid in his basement figuring it out, but it's a legitimate concern. And when this thing hits social media, there's no telling what sorts of eyes and minds might be analyzing it."

As she started to take a closer look at the letter, Finley came back in the room. "That was fast," O'Malley said.

"Well, it just so happens that one of the women on dispatch has a father that works near the Prudential Center. And that's within the 02199 zip code, by the way. Maybe just a coincidence, but you never know. Anyway, her husband works at a tech lab over that way. She says they do these crazy experiments with quantum mechanics and things like that. Some sort of arm of the tech school at Boston University."

"Quantum mechanics?" O'Malley asked. "That's doesn't fit with our guy, does it?"

"It depends on the experiments," Avery said, instantly interested. "I don't know much about the field, but I do know that there are areas in quantum mechanics that deal with extreme temperatures. Something to do with finding the durability and central origin points of different kinds of matter."

"How the hell do you know all of this?" Connelly asked.

She shrugged. "I watched a lot of Discovery Channel in college. Some of it stuck, I guess."

"Well, it's worth a shot," Connelly said. "Let's get some information on the lab and get out there to speak to the brass."

"I can get that done," Avery said.

"In the meantime," Connelly said, looking at his watch, "the nightly news goes live in about three minutes. Let's tune in and see how badly the media is going to fuck this case for us."

He stormed out of the conference room with O'Malley on his heels. Finley gave Avery an apologetic look and then followed out

26

after them. Ramirez looked at the letter over Avery's shoulder with a shake of the head.

"You think this guy is deranged or just wants us to *think* he's nuts?" he asked her.

"I'm not sure yet," she said, rereading the cryptic letter. "But I do know that this lab is the perfect place to start."

CHAPTER SEVEN

Esben Technologies was disguised among other normal-looking buildings about a mile and a half away from the Prudential Center, the block essentially a row of featureless gray buildings. Esben Technologies occupied the center building and looked exactly like the surrounding buildings—it hardly seemed like a lab.

As Avery stepped inside with Ramirez, she noticed the front lobby consisted of little more than a gorgeous wooden floor, highlighted by morning sun that poured in through a skylight overhead. A huge desk sat along the far wall. On one end, a woman was typing into a computer. On the other end, another woman was writing something down on a form of some kind. When Avery and Ramirez entered, this woman looked up and gave them a perfunctory smile.

"I'm Detective Avery Black and this is Detective Ramirez," Avery said as she approached the woman. "We'd like to have a word with whoever is in charge here."

"Well, the supervisor of the whole outfit lives in Colorado, but the man that sort of runs the ship here in the building should be in his office."

"He'll do just fine," Avery said.

"One moment," the receptionist said, getting to her feet and walking through a large oak door at the far side of the room.

When she was gone, Ramirez stepped close to Avery, keeping his voice low from the other woman who remained at the desk behind her laptop.

"Did you even know this place was out here before yesterday?" he asked.

"No clue. But I guess the low profile makes sense; technology centers that are tied to colleges but aren't actually on campus generally try to keep a low profile."

"More Discovery Channel?" he asked

"No. Good old research."

A little less than a minute passed before the woman returned. When she did, there was a man with her. He was dressed in a button-down shirt and khakis. A long white coat that resembled the sort doctors often wore partially covered it all. He wore an expression of worry and concern that seemed to be magnified by the glasses he wore.

28

"Hi there," he said, stepping toward Avery and Ramirez. He extended his hand for a shake and said, "I'm Hal Bryson. What can I do to help you?"

"You're the supervisor here?" Avery asked.

"More or less. There are only four of us that work here. We sort of rotate in and out but yes, I oversee the experiments and data."

"And what sort of work is done here?" Avery asked.

"Quite a lot," Bryson said. "At the risk of seeming demanding, if you could perhaps let me know why you've come here, I can probably be a bit more exact."

Avery kept her voice low, not wanting the women at the desk to hear her. And since it was clear that Bryson had no intention of inviting them back beyond the door to the lobby, she figured they'd have to just have the conversation right then and there.

"We're dealing with a case where a suspect seems to have an interest in ice and cold temperatures," she said. "He sent a taunting letter to the precinct yesterday. We're taking a chance to see if there might be some sort of research that goes on here that could be related. It's a very strange case so we're starting with the only clue we really have—the cold."

"I see," Bryson said. "Well, there are indeed a few experiments that take place here that involve extremely cold temperatures. I could take you back into the lab to show you but I'd have to insist that you are fully sanitized and put on the appropriate covering."

"I appreciate that," Avery said. "And maybe we will take you up on it later. Hopefully, we won't have to. Could you just give us the abridged version of some of these tests?"

"Of course," Bryson said. He seemed quite pleased to be able to help, taking on the manner of an expressive teacher as he started to explain things. "The bulk of tests and work we do here that involve frigid temperatures involves getting beyond what is known as the quantum back action limit. That limit is a temperature just barely above absolute zero—roughly ten thousand times colder than the temperatures you'd encounter in the vacuum of space."

"And what's the purpose of such work?" Avery asked.

"To aid in the research and development of hypersensitive sensors for more advanced work. It's also a great avenue to understanding the structure of certain elements and how they respond to such extreme temperatures."

"And you're able to reach those temperatures here in this building?" Ramirez asked.

"No, not in our labs. We're working as sort of an outreach for the National Institute of Standards and Technology in Boulder. We can get relatively close here, though."

"And you say there are only four of you," Avery said. "Has it always been that way?"

"Well, there were five of us until about a year ago. One of my colleagues had to step down. He was starting to have headaches and other health issues. He really just wasn't well."

"Did he step down of his own accord?" Avery asked.

"He did."

"And could we have his name, please?"

A little concerned now, Bryson said: "His name was James Nguyen. But please forgive me for saying so...I very seriously doubt he's the man you're after. He was always very kind, polite...a quiet man. Sort of a genius, too."

"I appreciate your candidness," Avery said, "but we have to follow up with whatever avenues are presented to us. Would you happen to know how we can get in touch with him?"

"Yes, I can get that information for you."

"When did you last speak with Mr. Nguyen?"

"It's been at least...oh, I don't know...eight months ago I'd say. Just a call to see how he was doing."

"And how *was* he doing?"

"Fine, as far as I know. He's working as an editor and researcher for a scientific journal."

"Thanks for your time, Mr. Bryson. If you could get Mr. Nguyen's contact information, that would be helpful."

"Sure," he said, looking rather sad. "One moment."

Bryson walked over to the receptionist behind the laptop and spoke quietly to her. She nodded and started typing something new. While they waited, Ramirez once again stepped in close to Avery. It was an odd feeling; to remain professional when he was standing so close was difficult.

"Quantum mechanics?" he said. "Vacuums in space? I think this one might be out of my league."

She smiled at him, finding it hard to not playfully kiss him. She did her best to stay focused as Bryson started back toward them with a printed slip of paper in his hand.

"It's above my head, too," she whispered to Ramirez, quickly flashing another smile at him. "But I sure don't mind swimming for the surface."

***

30

Some days, Avery was rather amazed at just how fluid and smooth things seemed to go. Bryson had given them the phone number, email address, and physical address for James Nguyen. Avery had placed a call to Nguyen and not only had he answered, but he had invited them to his home. He had seemed rather pleased to do so, in fact.

So when she and Ramirez walked to his front door forty minutes later, Avery couldn't help but get the feeling that they might be wasting their time. Nguyen lived in a gorgeous two-story house in Beacon Hill. Apparently, his career in science had paid dividends. Sometimes, Avery found herself in awe of people with mathematical and scientific minds. She loved to read texts by them or just listen to them speak (one of the reasons she had once been so drawn to things like the Discovery Channel and the *Scientific American* magazines she sometimes glanced through in the college library).

On the porch, Ramirez knocked on the door. It took no time for Nguyen to answer it. He appeared to be in his late fifties or so. He was dressed in a Celtics T-shirt and a pair of gym shorts. He looked casual, calm, and almost happy.

As they'd already introduced themselves on the phone, Nguyen invited them in. They entered an elaborate foyer that led into a large living area. It appeared that Nguyen had prepared for them; he had set out bagels and cups of coffee on what looked like a very expensive coffee table.

"Please, have a seat," Nguyen said.

Avery and Ramirez took a seat on the couch facing the coffee table while Nguyen sat down opposite them in an armchair.

"Help yourself," Nguyen said, gesturing to the coffee and bagels. "Now, what can I do for you?"

"Well, as I said on the phone," Avery said, "we spoke with Hal Bryson and he told us that you had to step down from your work with Esben Technologies. Could you tell us a bit about that?"

"Yes. Unfortunately, I was putting too much of my time and energy into my work. I started to get double vision and cluster headaches. I was working up to eighty-six hours a week for a stretch of about seven or eight months at one time. I just became obsessed with my work."

"With what aspect of the work, exactly?" Avery asked.

"Looking back, I honestly couldn't tell you," he said. "It was just knowing that we were so close to creating temperatures in the lab that could mimic what someone might feel in space. To find ways to manipulate elements with temperatures…there's something sort of godlike about it. It can get addicting. I simply didn't realize this until it was too late."

His obsession with his work certainly fits the description of whoever we're working for, Avery thought. Still, from just having spoken to Nguyen for a grand total of two minutes, she was pretty sure Bryson had been right. There was no way Nguyen was behind it.

"What exactly were you working on when you stepped down?" Avery asked.

"It's quite complicated," he said. "And since then, I've moved on from it. But essentially, I was working to get rid of the excess heat that is caused when atoms lose their momentum during the cooling process. I was tinkering with quantum units of vibration and photons. Now, as I understand it, it's been perfected by our folks in Boulder. But at the time, I was working myself *crazy!*"

"Outside of the work you're doing for the journal and things with the college, are you still doing any of the work?" she asked.

"I dabble here and there," he said. "But it's just things here at home. I have my own little private lab in a rental space a few blocks away. But it's nothing serious. Would you like to see it?"

Avery could tell that they weren't being baited or given false enthusiasm. Nguyen was clearly very passionate about the work he used to do. And the more he talked about what he had once done, the deeper they dug themselves into a world of quantum mechanics—something that was a world away from a crazed killer dumping a body in a freezing river.

Avery and Ramirez shared a look, which Avery ended with a nod. "Well, Mr. Nguyen," she said, "we truly appreciate your time. Let me leave you with one question, though: during the time you spent working in the lab, did you ever come cross anyone—coworkers, students, anyone—that struck you as eccentric or a little off?"

Nguyen took a few moments to think this over but then shook his head. "None that I can think of. Then again, us scientists are all a bit eccentric when you get right down to it. But if anyone pops into my head, I'll let you know."

"Thank you."

"And if you change your mind and think you'd like to see my lab, just let me know."

Passionate about his work and *lonely,* Avery thought. *Damn…that was me up until a few months ago.*

She could relate. And because of that, she gladly accepted Nguyen's business card when he offered it to her at the door. He closed the door as Avery and Ramirez made their way down the porch stairs and back to their car.

"Did you understand a single word that guy said?" Ramirez asked.

"Very little," she said.

But the truth was that he had said *one* thing that still clung to her mind. It did not make her think Nguyen was worth further investigation, but it did give her a new insight into how to think about their killer.

To find ways to manipulate elements with temperatures, Nguyen had said. *There's something sort of godlike about it.*

Maybe our killer is acting out some godlike fantasy, she thought. *And if he thinks he's godlike, he could be more dangerous than we think.*

CHAPTER EIGHT

The hamster looked like a furry block of ice when he took it out of the freezer. It *felt* like a block of ice, too. He couldn't help but giggle at the clink sound it made when he placed it on the cookie sheet. Its legs were sticking up in the air—a stark contrast to the way they had been pedaling back and forth in panic when he had first placed it in the freezer.

That had been three days ago. Since then, the police had discovered the girl's body in the river. He had been surprised at how far the body had made it. All the way to Watertown. And the girl's name had been Patty Dearborne. Sounded pretentious. But damn, that girl had been beautiful.

He thought idly of Patty Dearborne, the girl he had taken from the outskirts of the BU campus as he ran his finger along the hamster's frigid belly. He'd been so nervous, but it had been quite easy. Of course, he hadn't meant to kill the girl. Things had just gotten out of hand. But then…then it had all sort of unlocked for him.

Beauty could be taken, but not in any mortal sort of way. Even when Patty Dearborne had been dead, she'd still been beautiful. Once he had gotten Patty naked, he'd found the girl to be damn near flawless. There had been one mole on her lower back and a small scar along the upper part of her ankle. But other than that, she had been spotless.

He had dumped Patty in the river and when she'd hit the frigid water, she had been dead. He'd watched the news with great anticipation, wondering if they would be able to bring her back…wondering if the ice that had held her for those two days would preserve her in some way.

Of course, it had not.

I was sloppy, he thought, looking to the hamster. *It'll take some time, but I'll get it figured out.*

He was hoping the hamster might be part of it. With his eyes still on its little frozen body, he retrieved the two heating pads from the kitchen counter. They were the sort of warming pads used in athletics to loosen muscles and promote relaxation for strained parts of the body. He placed one of the pads beneath the body and the other over its stiff little legs and frigid underside.

He was sure it would take some waiting. He had plenty of time…he was in no real hurry. He was trying to cheat death and he knew death was not going anywhere.

With this thought in his head, he filled his apartment with a witch-like cackle. Giving the hamster one final look, he walked into his bedroom. It was quite tidy, as was the adjoining bathroom. He went into the bathroom and washed his hands with the efficiency of a surgeon. He then looked into the mirror and stared at his face—a face he sometimes thought of as a monster.

There was irreparable damage on the left side of his face. It started just below his eye and reached down to his bottom lip. While most of the skin and tissue had been salvaged in his youth, there was permanent scarring and discoloring on that side of his face. His mouth always seemed to be frozen in a permanent scowl as well.

At thirty-nine years of age, he had stopped caring about just how bad it looked. It was the hand he had been dealt. A shitty mother had resulted in a disfigured mess. But that was okay...he was working on fixing it. He looked to the mangled reflection in the mirror and smiled. It could take years to figure it out, but that was okay.

"Hamsters are only five bucks apiece," he said to the empty bathroom. "And those pretty college coeds are a dime a dozen."

He had done some reading, mainly in the forums of practicing nurses and med students. He figured if the experiment with the hamster was going to work, the heating pads needed to be on it for about forty minutes. It would be a slow thaw, one that would not too badly disrupt or shock the frozen heart.

He spent that forty minutes watching the news. He caught a few quick blips about Patty Dearborne. He learned that Patty was attending BU with aspirations of becoming a counselor. She'd had a boyfriend and currently had loving parents mourning her. He saw the parents on TV, hugging and crying together while speaking to the media.

He cut the TV off and walked into the kitchen. The smell of the thawing hamster was starting to fill the room...a smell he had not been expecting. He ran to the little body and threw the heating pads off of it.

The fur was singed and the previously frozen belly was slightly charred. He swiped the tiny furry body away. When it plopped onto the kitchen floor with little trails of smoke wafting from its hide, he screamed.

He stormed around the apartment for a while, furious. As was usually the case, his anger and absolute rage were driven by memories of an oven burner...blazing in his memories of childhood with the smell of burned flesh.

His screams downgraded to pouting and sobbing within five minutes. Then, as if nothing out of the ordinary had happened, he went into the kitchen and picked up the hamster. He tossed it into the garbage as if it were just a piece of trash and washed his hands at the kitchen sink.

He was humming by the time he was done. When he took his keys from the hook by the door, he habitually ran his free hand along the scarring along the left side of his face. He closed the door, locked up, and went down to the street. There, in the midst of an absolutely beautiful winter morning, he got into his red van and started down the road.

Almost casually, he glanced at himself in the rearview mirror.

That permanent scowl was still there, but he did not let that deter him.

He had work to do.

***

Sophie Lentz was done with this frat shit. For that matter, she was just about done with this college shit, too.

Vain or not, she knew how she looked. There were girls who were prettier than her, sure. But she had the Latin thing going for her, the dark eyes and raven black hair. She could also turn the accent on and off when she needed to. She'd been born in America, raised in Arizona, but according to her mother, the Latin had never left her. The Latin had never left her parents, either…not even when they had moved to New York the week after Sophie had been accepted into Emerson.

It was most apparent in her looks rather than her attitude and personality, though. And man, had that worked for her in Arizona. Honestly, it had worked for her in college, too. But only for her freshman year. She'd experimented then but not as badly as her mother was probably thinking. And apparently, word had gotten out: Sophie Lentz didn't take much prodding to get into bed and when she did land in your bed, buckle up because she was a firecracker.

She supposed there were worse reputations to have. But it had blown up in her face tonight. Some guy—she thought his name was Kevin—had started kissing her and she had let him. But when they were alone and he refused to take no for an answer…

Sophie's right hand still hurt. There was also still a bit of blood on her knuckle. She wiped it away on her tight jeans, recalling the sound of the asshole's nose crunching against her fist. She was

36

furious but, deep down, wondered if she sort of deserved it. She did not believe in karma but maybe the part of the vixen she had played last semester was catching up to her. Maybe she was reaping what she had sown.

She walked down the streets that cut through Emerson College, heading back to her apartment. Her goodie-goodie roommate would no doubt be studying for some test tomorrow, so at least she wouldn't be alone.

She was three blocks away from her apartment when she started to feel a strange sort of sensation. She looked behind her, sure that she was being followed, but there was no one. She could see the shapes of people in a little coffee bar a few feet behind her, but that was it. She had a fleeting irritated thought about what kind of morons drank coffee at 11:30 at night before she started on, still fuming over Kevin or whatever the guy's name had been.

Up ahead at a stoplight, someone was blaring some terrible hip-hop. The car's back bumper was rattling and the bass sounded wretched. *You're really being a bitch tonight, aren't you, slugger?* she said to herself.

She looked to her slightly swollen right hand and grinned. "Yes. Yes, I am."

By the time she reached the intersection where the booming car had been, the light had changed and the car raced off. She turned right at the intersection and her apartment building came into view. Again, though, she felt that creeping sensation. She turned to look behind her and again, nothing was there. A bit further down the street a couple was walking hand in hand. There were several cars parked along the street and a single red van driving down toward the stoplight she had just passed.

Maybe she was just being paranoid because some loser had basically tried to rape her. That plus the adrenaline that was flowing through her was an unhealthy combination. She just needed to get home, wash up, and get to bed. This partying crap had to stop.

She neared her apartment, really hoping her roommate wasn't home. She'd be asking tons of questions about why she was home early. She did it because she was nosy and didn't have a life of her own...not because she actually cared.

She made her way up the steps to the building. When she opened the door and stepped inside, she looked back down the street, feeling that sensation of being watched once again. The streets were empty, though; the only thing she saw was a couple making out furiously against the side of an apartment building three doors down. She also saw that same red van. It was parked at the stoplight, just sort of idling there. Sophie wondered if there was some horny dude driving it, watching the make-out session against the apartment building.

With a case of the creeps, Sophie headed inside. The door closed, leaving the night behind her. But that unsettling feeling remained.

***

She woke up when her roommate left the next morning. The noisy bitch was probably on her way out to get more mangoes or papayas for her pretentious fruit smoothies. Sophie was pretty sure her roommate had no classes this early today. She glanced at the clock and saw that it was 10:30.

Crap, she thought. She had class in an hour and there was no way she'd make it on time. She had to shower, throw some breakfast together, and then get to campus. She groaned, wondering how she'd let herself become this sort of girl. Was she going to be the tease now? Was she going to let her personal drama get in the way of her education and bettering her life? Was she—

A knock at the front door broke her out of her internal reflection. She grumbled and slipped out of bed. She was only wearing a pair of panties and a thin cotton T-shirt, but that didn't matter. This would almost certainly be her roommate. The idiot had probably left her wallet. Or keys. Or something...

Another knock, soft yet insistent. Yes...it would be her roommate. Only she had that sort of annoying knock.

"Hold your horses already," Sophie yelled.

She reached the door and answered it, unsetting the lock. She found herself looking at a stranger. There was something wrong with his face—that's the first thing she noticed.

And the last.

The stranger stormed into the apartment, closing the door quickly. Before Sophie could let out a scream, there was a hand at her throat and a cloth over her mouth. She breathed in a heavy dose of some sort of chemical—a scent that was so strong it made her eyes water as she fought against the stranger's grip.

Her fighting lessened quickly. By the time any real sort of fear had the chance to settle in, the world had gone a spinning shade of black that pulled Sophie down into something much darker and more final than sleep.

CHAPTER NINE

Nights that weren't crammed with work or in a state of hectic hurry were not something Avery was used to. So when she found herself in the middle of one, she was never quite sure how to respond. Currently, she was sitting on her couch, holding her phone and texting Rose. She knew that if she was truly going to keep Rose in her life from now on, she was going to have to make a point to make her a priority.

Yes, she had the case notes for the Patty Dearborne case in front of her but they were not consuming her. She also had a photocopy of the letter the killer had sent and while that kept taunting her, she did her best to place Rose above it all in that moment. In her texts to Rose, she was discovering that her daughter had been waiting for this sort of attention even if she wasn't aware of it. She was chit-chatting like a pre-teen girl, talking about boys and movies. They were also making plans for their next outing. Avery was very careful to also let Rose know what was going on with her workload so if something came up that would interfere with those plans, it wouldn't be out of the blue.

As Avery got accustomed to these weird conversation schematics with her nineteen-year-old daughter, she was also enjoying another aspect of her life that she had not quite gotten used to yet: having Ramirez over most of the time.

He was sitting on the opposite end of the couch, his legs outstretched. Their feet were tangled in one another, toes grazing lazily.

This is sort of sad, she thought. *Cute...but sad. I thought this part of my life was over...playing footsie with a handsome man on my couch. Is this my life now?*

She chuckled to herself. She couldn't help it. Sometimes the surprises life doled out were beyond comprehension.

Ramirez was also texting. Only his texts were a little more heated than Avery's. He was having a dispute with his landlord. It was a dispute that had been going on for the better part of two weeks now, as Ramirez's lease was about to expire and the landlord was asking for nearly one hundred dollars more for rent.

"Any luck?" she asked.

He looked up from his phone and shook his head. "No. I've even texted some other people in the building. He's only upping the rent on the ones on the higher floors, but almost everyone that is affected is willing to pay. It's just me and two other people that are griping about it."

"And when is the lease up?" she asked.

"Two weeks. Which means I need to find somewhere to live, pack my stuff up, and be ready to move pretty quickly."

"Any area you have in mind?"

"Yeah. My existing apartment. I love that place. I've been there for five years and now the landlord wants to pull this shit."

"Maybe we can make a Saturday of it this weekend. You and I will go apartment hunting and find you a nice place."

"Find me a place like *yours*, and you're on," he said.

She smiled as her phone dinged. It was Rose again. She wanted to know if they could catch a movie Saturday. Something dramatic but not cheesy. And no explosions of any kind. Avery texted her back, letting her know that it sounded like a great plan.

Beside her, Ramirez had set his phone down and started to sift through the case file on Patty Dearborne. She could tell that he was frustrated and maybe even a little tired. She figured he would be staying here tonight—it had been a general rule of thumb that he stayed over any afternoon where he hadn't left by seven or so. And that was fine with Avery. She liked having him around. And it was more than just the steady conversation, the easy access to sex, and the help in the kitchen. It had been far too long since she had consistently shared a space with someone. She was starting to get back into the habit and it felt good. The way things were going with Ramirez and Rose as of late was a stark reminder of what life *could* be like. It didn't have to be work all of the time, nor a need to constantly beat herself up. She was only slightly beyond forty; she still had most of her figure, her looks, and an exciting career. There was no reason to assume the best parts of her life were over when there was so much still waiting ahead.

"Hey, so I have a thought," Avery said, setting her phone down and looking at Ramirez.

"What's that?" he said, still looking at the case files.

"Instead of apartment hunting this weekend, why don't we just go over to your place and pack everything up?"

"Because I'd like to know where I'm moving it to before I box it all up," he said. He looked up from the case files, clearly confused.

"Well, I have an idea on that. Why not just move it in here?"

A smile slowly crept onto his face. He narrowed his eyes at her in a comical look and set the file back down on the coffee table. "What?"

40

"Move in with me," she said.

"Um, well, I'd love to. But are you sure? We see each other almost all day at work. You wouldn't get sick of me if you had to come home with me, too?"

She scooted over to him, closing the distance between them on the couch. She placed a soft kiss on his mouth and shook her head. "No, I would not. And yes, I'm sure."

"I don't know," he said. "I mean, I'd love to. It could be amazing. I just don't want to ruin what we've got."

"So don't," she said.

She then threw her right leg over so that she was straddling him while he sat. It was a playful pose as she sat her rear down on his knees and faced him. That was another great thing about him; he made her feel playful, joyful, and sexy.

"Let's discuss it and figure it out," he said. "I think we can make it work, but I think we need to talk it out."

"Okay," she said. "But later."

With that, she reached down to the hem of her shirt and lifted it up over her head. As she tossed the shirt on the floor, Ramirez pulled her closer. His hands went to her back, unfastening her bra, and after that, there was very little talking for the next hour or so.

CHAPTER TEN

Norman Behrens didn't know why, but he had always thought there was something very cool about being able to just leave his beer in the back of the pickup truck and knowing it would be cold when he retrieved one. He'd put the case in the cooler two hours ago and it was already cold. He could feel it even through his gloves.

He popped the top on his can of Budweiser and took a drink from it. Following the cooler, he then removed the other items in the back of his truck: two fishing rods, a smaller cooler with a container of minnows, and his handheld drill.

Beside him, his friend Weldon Smith plucked a beer from the cooler as well. He also took one of the fishing rods. The two men chuckled and tapped their beer cans together.

"You sure about this?" Weldon asked.

"No," Norman said. "But I never tried it and we don't have much of anything else to do, now do we?"

Both men looked out toward the small grove of trees ahead of them. Norman had parked his truck on the side of a dirt road that only state employees were supposed to be able to use. But he had long ago copied that key, having swiped it from a guy that worked down at the pump station. That very same station sat less than two miles away, on the other side of the Fresh Pond Reservoir. On the other side of the trees ahead of them, the reservoir shone like a quarter. Moonlight bounced from the iced-over water beautifully as the two men made their way through the trees.

Technically, they were trespassing. And they would *definitely* be trespassing after they crossed those trees. But Norman had been out here before. The dirt road he had parked on was an awesome place to deer hunt and he had always wanted to try fishing in the reservoir. Because it was so damned cold, he knew security would be lax and hey…throwing *ice* into the fishing equation was just one more challenge as far as Norman Behrens was concerned.

They made it out to the edge of the concrete barrier that separated the reservoir from the grounds of the surrounding stretch of thin woodland. They walked quietly, the only sound coming from the aluminum cans slapping together in the cooler. They stopped at the edge of the concrete and walked along the boundary, heading to the far end where there were more shadows created by the trees. Out here, there was no way in hell anyone would catch them.

Norman stopped walking and Weldon simply stood there, waiting.

"Okay," Weldon said. "Get out on that ice. I still don't think it's strong enough to hold us."

"Yeah it is," Norman said. "Kids have been ice skating on it for the last few days. Watch."

Norman took a deep breath and cautiously stepped out on the ice. He held his beer in one hand and the handheld drill in the other. It *did* feel a little thin but he heard no cracks and the ice did not pitch or sink when he stepped out on it. He took a few experimental steps further out, growing more and more confident by the minute.

He looked back at Weldon and smiled. He then raised his beer and took a long gulp. He hunkered down on his knees, set his beer to the side, and adjusted the drill bit. As he pressed the trigger on the drill and started boring into the ice, Weldon also summoned up the nerve to come out on the ice. He carried both rods and the small bucket of minnows, which they would use as bait. Neither of them had any idea what sort of fish they'd catch out here. Nor did they really care. It was an excuse to do something fun. An excuse to drink and take home a cool story.

"I'll be damned," Weldon said. "Looks like you were right."

"I told you," Norman said over the whir of the drill. "It's been too cold for it to—"

They could hear the cracking noise even over the sound of the drill. Right away, Weldon started to backpedal toward the concrete lip of the reservoir. Norman let go of the drill's trigger and looked to the left where a huge crack had zigged and zagged its way through the ice.

"Damn," he said, slowly getting up.

When he was back on his feet, the ice slid to the left, pitching a bit in the water. And then another crack ran through it, this one going directly between his feet and springing out of the hole he had drilled.

Weldon was already back on the concrete, looking out like a man waiting for a disaster. "You better get your ass over here!" he yelled.

I know, I know, Norman thought nervously. If he fell in this water, he'd never hear the end of it.

Holding his drill tightly, he walked as quickly as he could across the fractured ice. With each step, it cracked more and more, now accompanied by a groaning sound. With scary speed, he felt the ice growing weaker and weaker; he could feel himself bobbing up and down.

He felt ice water creep across the toes of his boots and he knew he had to jump. If he didn't, the ice would break apart and he'd go in the water. With about three feet separating him from the concrete, he jumped.

He almost made it.

His drill went clattering across the concrete as his body from the waist up hit the concrete. The rest of him went splashing into the water. He let out a little wail of surprise as his legs were soaked in ice cold water.

Weldon helped him onto the concrete, but he was laughing hysterically. He had even dropped his beer during the whole fiasco and didn't seem to know.

"Shut it, Weldon," Norman said as he got to his feet on the concrete. His feet were freezing and he was beyond embarrassed. He'd been wrong about the ice after all.

"Shit," Weldon said. "Norman—look at that."

Weldon's face had gone pale—looking like *he* had been the one to fall in the water.

He was pointing into the reservoir, into the icy water that had just about taken Norman. Norman followed his friend's finger and saw nothing at first. But then it was unmistakable.

Something was floating in the dark water. It was pale and barely moving at all. As Norman saw it, a sheet of ice coasted into it and bounced off. Norman knew what he was seeing, but his mind refused to accept it. But then he saw the bare breasts and it seemed to snap him back toward logic.

"Oh my God," Norman said.

Both men fell silent as they watched the body listlessly float in the water, staring eternally up at the sky.

44

CHAPTER ELEVEN

When it was clear that the couch was not going to allow them to become as active as they liked to be, they moved to the bedroom. It was there, amid a jumble of sheets and candlelight, that they finally started talking again.

"What will Rose think if I move in?" Ramirez asked.

"I don't know," Avery answered. "I'll talk to her about it. But the fact that you're even concerned about it makes me want you to move in a little more. It also makes me think you might be getting Round Two tonight before we go to sleep."

"I have to say…it would be a weird dynamic. Not only would we be working together as partners *and* living together—but if you take this sergeant position, I'd also be living with my boss."

"Well, let's be real," she said, playfully reaching below the sheets and seizing him gently. "I'm sort of the boss here already."

"Touché," he said. "But in all seriousness, I think you should take it. You know that O'Malley and Connelly already basically come to you as if you already had the position anyway. They think a hell of a lot of you."

She only nodded because even though it was true, it was still hard for her to verbally admit it.

"I do, too, you know," he said.

"I know."

It was a conceited thought, but she was pretty certain Ramirez was in love with her. She supposed she loved him, too. But with their jobs and the things they saw on a daily basis, that was one word neither of them was ready to approach yet. Avery had only said it to two people in her entire life. One had been a stupid boy in ninth grade and the second had been her husband. It was just a dumb word, but she knew how much it changed things when it was tossed out there.

Ramirez rolled over onto his back and Avery sidled up next to him. She rested her head on his shoulder and placed an arm around him. She had joked about Round Two but she didn't think it would happen. They were both content and it was nearing ten o'clock. They both liked to wake up early and although the sex was the best she'd ever had, even sex sometimes wasn't as satisfying as a good night's sleep.

Round Two was efficiently ruled out ten minutes later when Ramirez fell asleep. She knew he wouldn't stir again until morning. It was something she teased him about—how he could just fall asleep right away without brushing his teeth. She was the polar opposite, which was why she got out of bed, draped herself in her robe, and headed into the bathroom. She brushed her teeth and looked out into the bedroom. She loved the way his sleeping shape looked beneath the sheets and knew right then and there that she did want him to live with her.

She finished up with her teeth, threw on a pair of underwear and a T-shirt, and started back toward her bed. As she went, though, she paused at her window. She looked out, staring into the thin stretch of Boston skyline in the distance. Down below and to her right, she could see just a tiny fraction of the Charles River. It sparkled in ice and streetlights, the small bend of water she had always seen from this view in her bedroom. Now, though, having seen a body pulled from it, it was hard to see the water as anything resembling pretty.

She looked at the water, visualizing the way it looked year-round; spring turned the water into a mirror of the blooming vegetation along its banks, the summer made it a murky promise of cooling, the fall made it the meandering brooks of calendars, and the winter turned it into a frosty staple of cold weather. It could be appealing to just about anyone in those four stages. But what would draw a killer to it in the winter? A sense of desolation? A sense of things coming to an end?

Will he use the Charles River again? she wondered.

Realizing that sleep was not going to come anytime soon, she crept back out to the living room and sat down with the case files. She started by going back over everything she knew about Patty Dearborne. She had been a BU student, majoring in psychology. Twenty-two years old—three years older than Rose. No record, no apparent enemies, a stand-up young lady. Church-goer, tutored in her spare time. Apparently, she had just been in the wrong place at the wrong time.

Or had she? She was beautiful, unblemished. Even in the cold...

Something about that struck her as odd…as motive almost.

She then looked to the letter the killer had sent. She read it and reread it, staring at it as if it were some piece of art to be deciphered and understood on a deeper level. She analyzed the words that seemed to stick out the most. *Windshield. Erotic. Flower.* She started to wonder if it might be worth contacting a Lit professor or maybe someone with a deep knowledge of the constructs of word usage and poetry.

She also looked at her phone, pulling up an email that had come in earlier in the afternoon. So far, there had been no luck in finding a source of information on the hacking of the elderly woman's email account that had been used to send the letter to the media.

Still...someone with enough knowledge to hack into someone's email account and *a killer's mindset that just happens to be drawn toward ice. This is going to make for a fairly difficult profile...*

Usually by this point in a case, she was able to at least get some sort of grasp on the killer's mentality. This would allow her to view the case from the killer's eyes, opening up new avenues to search for leads.

But she was unable to find a way in so far. This killer was unique in a way she had never seen before.

He wants to be known...maybe even eventually caught. Hacking an email address, writing a letter, shaving and meticulously cleaning the victim. It speaks of planning, of patience, and a structure to his madness.

Feeling herself at a roadblock of sorts, Avery gave in after a while. She returned to the bedroom and slid into bed beside Ramirez. Just as she pulled the covers up around her, the room was filled with the all-too-familiar noise of her cell phone ringing. As she reached for it on her nightstand, Ramirez let out a little groan of disappointment from the bed.

"This is Avery," she said.

"Hey, Avery," said a man's voice. "This is Finley, calling for O'Malley. Sorry to call so late."

If they're getting him to go up the ladder, they need to teach him to get to the point, Avery thought.

"It's okay, Finley. What is it?"

"Bundle up," he said with a morbid chuckle. "We need you out here. We've got another body."

CHAPTER TWELVE

For the second time in three days, Avery found herself driving outside of Boston to reach a crime scene. This time, the body had been discovered in Cambridge at the Fresh Pond Reservoir. The night seemed even darker that usual thanks to the unforgiving cold. She and Ramirez pulled in behind several other police cars, most of which belonged to Cambridge PD.

Great, Avery thought. *Just what we need...a turf war between the police. Maybe they'll be as hospitable as the PD from Watertown.*

She quickly located familiar faces in the crowd of a dozen or so police. Finley and O'Malley were speaking with a man in a police uniform. When O'Malley spotted her, he waved her over with a sense of urgency. Avery bustled over with her hands stuffed in her pockets. It was cold as hell out tonight; her phone had read twelve degrees when she and Ramirez had stepped out to respond to the call.

"Avery," O'Malley said. "Meet Chief Tagart. This is his show out here in Cambridge but he's agreed to let you have first run before his guys get in there and busy up the scene."

"That's right," Tagart said. "Even I can see the similarities in that God-awful case with the Dearborne girl. So do what you can. Just...remember whose district you're in."

"Got it," she said a little rudely. She hated nothing more than for a man in power to make a sad power play when it was clear that he wanted nothing to do with the problem. Especially when that man was faced with a woman who was more skilled than he was. Still, she knew how to make things work their smoothest, so she wasn't going to rock the boat.

She walked out to the ice with Ramirez still behind her. "You okay?" he asked.

"Yeah, I'll be good. If this case isn't closed soon, I'll be something of an expert at ice skating."

The joke fell flat as she reached the edge of the reservoir and saw that the body had already been retrieved from the ice. She tried not to get too pissed about this, though; from what she could tell, the corpse had been handled carefully. She saw a young woman, maybe eighteen to twenty years of age. Like Patty Dearborne, she was completely naked and, even in frigid death, looked quite striking.

48

Two officers were by the body—a man taking notes and a sad-looking woman taking pictures. "You Detective Black?" the woman asked.

"Yes," Avery said, reaching for her ID.

"Good riddance," the woman said. "This whole scene makes me sick. It's all yours."

With a saddened look, the woman started back up the bank toward the bubble lights of the gathered police cars.

Avery hunkered down by the body, already placed on top of a tarp. She got a closer look at the girl using a small Maglite she took from her coat pocket. As she had suspected, there was not a speck of hair on this girl below the head. Again, there was no jewelry although Avery could clearly see an indentation on her pinky and right ring finger where rings had been until recently. She saw no bruises, no blood...nothing.

She hated to do it, but she stared down at the body to compare and contrast this one with the body of Patty Dearborne. She tried her best to slip out of detective mode and into the mind of a man that would hunt this type of women. She saw no obvious signs of sexual assault, though that could not be ruled out without a thorough medical exam. And in cases like this, when you removed the sexual aspect as motive, it left far too many questions.

She studied the body, starting to feel twinges of the sadness and sickness the woman who had just walked away had described.

Patty Dearborne had blonde hair, while this new body had dark black hair. Patty had been a typical white American girl while a first glance at this new girl indicated some sort of Latin heritage. This girl had smaller breasts whereas Patty Dearborne's had been much fuller and larger than average. Other than those differences, there was nothing.

"Ramirez," she said, remembering that he was behind her.

"Yeah?"

"Can you get me some evidence gloves?"

He didn't say anything but did as she asked right away. While he was gone, Avery looked at the girl again and sorted through her thoughts.

Both were young girls. Dearborne was a college student at BU. I'd put money on this girl also being a student. First glance shows no signs of violence, so there was likely no struggle or, if there was, it was minimal. Two very attractive girls, both very small in stature. Dearborne's weight at death was one hundred and ten. This girl looks even smaller. The killer has some weird fixation on beauty...and apparently ice. A weird combination for sure...

49

"Here you go," Ramirez said, returning behind her. He handed her a pair of evidence gloves and when she took them, she gave him a nod of appreciation. She slipped them on and then searched the body a bit more.

She started with the hair, pulling it lightly part and looking at the scalp for any indication of head trauma. Forensics had not come up with anything like that for Patty Dearborne, but she wanted to eliminate it from the start.

She then carefully rolled the girl onto her side. Again, there was no sign of violence. There was a very small tattoo on this girl's lower back, one of those generic Chinese symbols that probably didn't mean what the victim had thought it meant. She rested the girl on her back again and then lifted up her hands. If there had been any sort of a struggle, there might be some sort of sign on the palms or fingers.

Again, nothing.

Shit, Avery thought. *Nothing to go on. Other than beauty, what would draw the killer to these two girls? Maybe he hates beauty. But that doesn't feel right because he's going out of his way to make them clean, hairless, perfect. Is he capturing them with intent to act out sexual fantasies and then being tormented by guilt and fear? Is he perhaps paying tribute to them by making them so clean and flawless? I mean, this girl is spotless...*

But then she saw the very slight abnormality on the girl's left pointer finger. The fingernail had been finely polished like the others but there was the slightest little crack in it. More than that, there was a very small piece of fabric clinging to the crack.

It was a very minor find but at least it was *something.*

Avery heard more footsteps approaching. She turned and saw O'Malley and Chief Tagart heading in her direction. "What do you think, Black?" O'Malley asked.

"I think we need Forensics down here. This girl is in the exact same shape as Patty Dearborne, but there's a very small bit of fabric clinging to a tear in this girl's fingernail. It might turn out to yield absolutely nothing, but it's the only scrap of evidence we have."

"Forensics is about five minutes out. Anything else?"

"Beauty and ice. Those are our guy's triggers. Chief Tagart, do you know anything about the security camera setup around here?"

"There are a few cameras, but that's near the front of the property. You know, Fresh Pond used to be a park but it eventually just became a reservoir. I've already got some men speaking to security to get a look at the footage, but hopes aren't very high."

"I don't get it," O'Malley said. "Stripped naked. Young, pretty girls. And there are zero signs of abuse or rape?"

"Zero," Avery agreed. "We need a thorough medical exam to confirm, but I feel confident this body will yield the same results as Patty Dearborne—so signs of sexual assault."

"What's your gut say?" O'Malley asked.

"Everything you just said in addition to the riddle-like letter points to a killer that has a purpose—a purpose they can see clearly. But it also points to the very real possibility of someone suffering from a mental break of some sort. Taking women like this for sexual fantasies or abuse of some kind is driven by an impulse or deep-seated physical need. But to do this so systematically—the shaving, the cleanliness—points to someone that might be—"

"—fucking crazy?" Tagart asked.

Avery nodded, wincing. "I was going to say potential guilt, fear, or disgust. Maybe a man that wants the women for sex at first but then bails out."

Tagart shrugged, as if he either didn't really care or was done listening.

"Anything else?" O'Malley asked.

"Yes. Given the timeline of these two bodies being discovered and the methodical approach," she said wearily, "I can guarantee that there will be more bodies to come."

CHAPTER THIRTEEN

Due to the late hour, the subsequent meeting at the A1 was a small one. That was fine with Avery; she actually preferred it that way. At 1:10 in the morning, she sat at the head of the table with a cranky-looking Connelly to her left. O'Malley sat next to him, then there was Finley and then Ramirez at the end of the table. A few of the guys from Forensics were also in the building but they were hard at work in the lab, doing what they could to work with the Cambridge guys to come up with something—anything—that could provide a solid lead on the case.

The one bit of information they did have on the latest body had come from fingerprints. The girl's name was Sophie Lentz. She was a nineteen-year-old Emerson College sophomore. A pair of officers were currently out on duty to inform Sophie's roommate. Based on college records, her parents lived in New York, having moved there right after Sophie got into Emerson. This was a minor relief to Avery, as she would not be involved with informing the family.

The current meeting was not an actual meeting, as there was no new information to go over. Avery knew it was really just a gathering to await any results Forensics might turn up. Still, she thought it best to keep their minds active and sharp so she did her best to recap what they knew without being redundant.

"I think this might be some form of art for our killer," Avery said. "The absolute nature of it—the cleanliness, the shaving, the lack of jewelry. And we know Sophie Lentz had jewelry on because the indentations are on her fingers from where she was wearing rings."

"But if it's art," O'Malley said, "why is he creating it only to destroy it?"

"Maybe the deaths are part of the art," Avery suggested. "The fact that both of these girls were quite pretty, nude, and show no signs of rape or other abuse makes me go to the exact opposite end of the spectrum. He is not taking these women for any sort of physical pleasure. There's something more to it for him. It's almost like a respect thing. That or like I said at the reservoir, it could be a guilt thing. He could be disposing of them out of guilt. Guilt and disgust are the only driving factors I can think of that might cause a man to take these beautiful girls and then dispose of them after cleaning them. He doesn't want them for sex because maybe he has some sort of aversion to it."

Connelly wrote some of this down on a legal pad in front of him. "The first one was from BU and now this one from Cambridge," he said. "So there's no one specific area he's targeting."

"And the bodies are turning up in an even wider area," Avery pointed out. "Watertown to Cambridge."

A knock at the door had all of them turning in sync. Two familiar faces from Forensics came into the room—a seasoned vet named Amy Reed and the resident science nerd by admission, a young guy named Christopher Paulson. Amy was carrying a series of printed pages and from the look on her face, Avery assumed they had found something.

"Two things for you," Amy said, walking to the head of the table and wasting no time. "First, the little fragment of cloth we found on her fingernail...which, by the way, it's a miracle it wasn't washed away when she went into the water. It was so damn cold that it sort of froze on as well as clung to the small tear in her fingernail. Anyway...there was nothing notable about the material itself. It was just a basic washcloth. However, when we analyzed the bit of fabric, we found trace amounts of household bleach as well as acetone."

"Homemade chloroform," Avery said.

"Exactly," Amy said.

"What was the second thing?" Connelly asked.

"The tattoo on her lower back," Christopher said. "There were trace amounts of bleach there as well. While her entire body appeared to have been cleaned, there was a slight redness to the skin around the tattoo. Closer analysis reveals that the area had been scrubbed heavily, as if the killer was trying to remove it."

"That's it?" Connelly asked.

Amy gave him a slight frown and nodded. "Yes. That's all we had to go on at one o'clock in the morning."

Sensing a cranky and tired Connelly on the brink of being an asshole, Avery took the papers from Amy. "Thanks so much, Ms. Reed. This is great."

"Any time," Amy said. She gave Avery a smile as she and Christopher took their leave without glancing back at Connelly.

When the door was closed, Avery scanned the printouts from the lab. Most of it went over her head but she still liked to have as much information as possible.

"Chloroform," she said. "So at least now we know how he's getting his victims."

"Yeah, but is that lethal?" Finley asked.

"In high doses, it can be," Avery said. "It's also pretty quick and efficient if it is ingested. Add to the mix that this was a homemade batch and that makes it even deadlier."

"It's worth pointing out that the art theory looks a little more likely now," Ramirez said. "Someone tried to scrub that tattoo off. But if they wanted it off bad enough, they could have just sliced the skin off."

"It also says that our killer isn't too smart," Avery said. "To think you could scrub a tattoo off speaks of either low intelligence or some sort of break with reality."

"And what about the ice?" O'Malley said. "Is that a solid link?"

"I'm leaning towards yes," Avery said. "The cold makes the skin pale, almost wax-like. There's also the cryptic letter he sent us where he actually refers to ice directly."

"Well, I hate to break it to you all," Connelly said, getting up and rubbing at his eyes. "We're not getting a break in this cold weather for several weeks. So this asshole has a virtual paradise on his hands if we don't nab him soon."

A brief silence passed through the room, broken when Ramirez got to his feet and clapped his hands loudly a single time. "Right then," he said. "I guess I'll put some coffee on."

Avery appreciated the effort. Sure, it was nearing 1:30 in the morning, but this was a job that sometimes just didn't give a damn about a sleep schedule. She watched Ramirez leave the conference room and when he did, she thought about the conversation they'd had before receiving the call about a body being discovered at Fresh Pond Reservoir.

I've sat on this long enough, she thought timidly. *And is there really a better time than while in the midst of a case that's kicking our asses?*

"Finley, I'd like a word with Connelly and O'Malley in private, please."

Finley looked to the two men and they gave him a little nod. When Finley left the room, she noticed he looked a little relieved. She was pretty sure he wasn't too accustomed to working such late hours. Whatever wringer O'Malley and Connelly were putting him through, they were pushing it hard.

Avery spoke up the moment Finley closed the door. She felt that if she didn't, she might quickly change her mind.

"I'd like to officially accept the sergeant position," she said.

Connelly smiled for the first time of the night—maybe for the first time all week as far as Avery knew. "Glad to hear it," he said.

54

"That's fantastic," O'Malley agreed. "You're going to bring a whole new level of intensity to it. I can't wait."

"Of course," O'Malley said, "you'll need to take the sergeant exam but you'll ace that."

"I'll start pushing the paperwork part tomorrow during normal hours," Connelly said. "There'll be a transition period of about two weeks or so, but we can handle all of that later. Seriously, Black...I'm glad you made this decision."

"Me, too," Avery said.

When the conference room door opened up, Avery was hoping it would be Ramirez. She wanted to share the news with him as soon as possible. But it was Amy who came through the door, again with an excited look on her face.

"I think I might have a lead for you," Amy said, standing in the doorway. "There was a very slight spot of discoloration on the back of Sophie Lentz's knee. We thought nothing of it, as it was no bigger than a pea. But we received her medical reports about five minutes ago via email and found that she visited a dermatologist about two weeks ago to have a lesion removed from the back of her knee."

"So?" Connelly said.

"So, the lesion was removed using cryosurgery—using liquid nitrogen to freeze warts, lesions, and skin abnormalities. And the doctor that performed it...well, let's just say he doesn't have the best reputation."

"And that's a solid lead," Avery said, taking out her phone and typing in the notes. "Thanks, Amy. Could you send me the doctor's information?"

Amy gave a spunky thumbs-up as she left the room. Directly after she was gone, Ramirez came walking back in. "Coffee's brewing," he said.

Skin abnormalities, she thought. *Removing them with ice...for someone that is not in the medical profession, could it be almost symbolic? Maybe even hopeful? Is the killer thinking he is saving these women by killing and freezing them? One way or the other, that's a very promising lead.*

"Just in time," O'Malley said, smiling at Ramirez. He then looked at Avery and added: "You can let him know, too. But it can't be public knowledge for another few days."

"What?" Ramirez asked. But no sooner did he ask the question than a thin smile crept onto his face. He looked to Avery, his eyes beaming. "Sergeant Black," he said, unable to keep in a chuckle.

"More importantly," Avery said, "Amy just brought us the first real lead on this case."

"But it's a lead you won't be able to pursue until morning," O'Malley pointed out. "Look, I'm not stupid. Get home and celebrate this promotion. But make sure you're well rested and beating on the door of this lead first thing in the morning."

Ramirez chuckled again and took a seat. "She's going to be a sergeant soon," he said. "You should probably know her a little better by now."

"What do you mean?" O'Malley asked.

"He means it's two in the morning and we just got a lead on this case," Avery said. "There's no way I'm going back home to sleep...or do anything else."

She thought she caught Ramirez blushing a bit as he shrugged. O'Malley and Connelly thankfully remained quiet as she started going through the case files. She bit back a smile, feeling a weird sort of camaraderie pass between them—a feeling she had been missing among her superiors for quite a while. It was nice. It was enough to make her think that she had definitely made the right decision in being promoted to sergeant.

But the pictures in the case files did not let her dwell on that success for long. In the file, pictures of the frozen Charles River (soon to be joined with pictures of the frozen Fresh Pond Reservoir) loomed dark and foreboding, as if begging her to chisel away at the ice to find the secrets hiding beneath.

She thought of her new lead, the dermatologist, and it all seemed to come together.

He might just be the killer.

CHAPTER FOURTEEN

Deckler Dermatology was located just six blocks from A1 headquarters. It was the sort of building Avery passed every day but paid no real attention to. It was located in a fairly nice part of town but the building was easily one of the worst in the area. The exterior was a bit of a mess, a fresh coat of paint barely salvaging the old crumbling brick. The interior was a little better but not much. There was a general office sort of smell to the place, made no better by the generic paintings on the waiting room wall.

"I don't think I'd come here willingly," Ramirez whispered to her as they sat down to wait to speak to Dr. Eric Deckler.

"Look around," she said, indicating the four other people in the waiting room. Two were clearly college-aged kids. Another was an older woman dressed in ratty clothes, probably forced to visit this particular dermatologist by rigid insurance regulations. "I don't think it's the first choice for anyone…just a necessity."

She tried to think about nineteen-year-old Sophie Lentz coming here with an appointment to have her lesion removed. A college kid without a lot of money. A place like this might be all she could afford. It was an easy scenario to picture, as Sophie had been the same age as Rose.

They had been sitting down for a little less than ten minutes when the waiting room door opened. A nurse waved them in her direction, trying her best to be discreet. They both got up and walked across the waiting room. After the nurse ushered them into a hall and closed the door behind them, she led them to the end of the hall and to an office. She did all of this without saying a word. It seemed incredibly suspicious as far as Avery was concerned. But she supposed it made sense, considering some of the charges that had been brought against Dr. Deckler in the past couple of years.

In the office, Eric Deckler sat behind a messy desk. His hands were folded in front of him and he looked at Avery and Ramirez with a scowl. He made no attempt to hide the fact that he was annoyed by their presence.

"And what is it this time?" he asked.

Avery took a seat in the chair in front of his desk without being invited to do so. "Dr. Deckler, that's not really the way you want to start out this morning, now is it?"

"I don't know yet," he spat. "This is the third unprompted and totally unnecessary visit I've had from the police in the last six months. It's growing a little old."

"We're here to ask about a patient that you saw two weeks ago by the name of Sophie Lentz."

"I'm sure you know that I can't share information with you regarding patients," Deckler said. He spoke it as if he had said it many times before, using it as a shield of sorts.

"Oh yes, I absolutely understand that," Avery said. "However, the case sort of changes when the patient shows up dead, her naked body pulled from a reservoir."

Avery watched Deckler's face, knowing that any guilt or fear would show in the moments after such a revelation. But she saw nothing. If anything, he seemed a bit shocked and taken aback.

"And I'm connected just because she was a patient of mine?"

"In a perfect world, no," Avery said. "But that perfect world would not include your sordid history. A history that includes allegations of sexual misconduct with your patients as well as a stalking charge from ten months ago—a charge filed by a former patient."

"I was found innocent in both cases, as you damn well know," Deckler said. "Otherwise, my license would have been revoked. And believe me, I've paid the price. There's been a significant drop in my number of patients and unless something changes, I'll likely have to close my practice by the middle of next year."

"With all due respect," Avery said, "I'm not interested in your sob story. I know about the allegations against you and yes, I am aware you were found innocent. But in my profession, I also know that where there is smoke, there is fire. I go where the lead takes me and right now, it has brought me to you."

"Well, what exactly do you need to know?"

"If you can provide alibis for your nights for the last week or so, we'll be done here."

"And do you have any idea how insulting this is?"

Avery shrugged, waiting for him to provide an answer. As she waited, her phone buzzed from within her pocket. She checked it and saw that she had a message from Connelly. She read it and knew that the next five minutes could indeed be very interesting. The message read:

Just got info from Patty Dearborne's parents. She saw Deckler three months ago to have a wart removed from her heel. Bring him in.

Returning the phone to her pocket, Avery asked: "Do you recall a patient by the name of Patty Dearborne?"

"I see too many patients to remember their names," Deckler said.

58

"Even the really pretty college girls?"

"This is going beyond insulting!"

"Well, I hate to tell you that it's about to get worse. The text I just received from my supervisor has instructed me to bring you in because of another link. We can do it quietly, or we can take you out through the waiting room while causing a fuss."

"You bitch," he hissed.

Ramirez stepped forward behind her but she knew it wouldn't come to that. Deckler was too worried about his reputation. He wasn't going to cause a scene when just one more bad news story could result in his practice closing down much earlier than he expected.

Avery stood and gestured toward the door. "Shall we?"

Deckler got to his feet like he was about to storm a battlefield. "You enjoying this? Is that it?"

"Dr. Deckler, there are two dead young women and no guilty party behind bars. So no...I am very far from enjoying this. Now get your ass through that door."

***

They were back at the precinct at 9:20. The media presence was still lingering, still salivating over the absurdity of the letter the killer had sent out yesterday. Avery did her best to remain as nonconfrontational as she could, opting to take Deckler in through the rear entrance, where the media could not get without passing security.

Finley met them at the back and escorted Deckler into the building. Avery and Ramirez followed after them but were stopped by Connelly halfway down the hall. He looked a bit more relaxed and calmer than he had last night but that really said nothing.

"Black, I need a word with you," he said. "Ramirez, can you see what you can do to help Finley out?"

Ramirez gave a nod and headed off to do his duty. Avery, meanwhile, followed Connelly further down the hallway and into his office. When he was sitting down behind his desk and in his element, he started to seem like a totally different person. She'd noticed it about him in the past; he seemed more grounded when he was sitting behind a desk, looking over at someone else.

"Things are going to be getting crazy over the next few days," Connelly said. "There's just no avoiding it. Your sergeant's exam is scheduled for next Tuesday. I can give you a list of the things you

59

need to study but I honestly think you'll blow it out of the water. Any questions there?"

"None for right now," she said.

"Okay. So here's the next thing. We're bringing a rookie into the A1. Well...not a rookie per se. She's been a beat cop and is coming on here as a detective. We're hoping she'll eventually take your place once you have transitioned into the role of sergeant. I know it's a lot to ask, but I'd like for her to come alongside of you. It probably won't be for this case, but the next one for sure. I'd like to say I could ask your opinion on this one, but it's already been decided."

Avery hated the idea. While she had no problem helping to bring up the next generation of detectives for the A1, she knew that there were a lot of responsibilities in training a rookie. Still, she nodded and said: "I'm sensing there's a third thing?"

"There is," he said. "Sophie Lentz's parents are in town. They arrived about half an hour ago, staying with a family friend until after Sophie's funeral. I'd really like for you to get over there and talk to them. We'll grill Deckler here. I'd rather you speak with the family."

"I can do that," she said, not particularly caring for the idea. "Anything else?"

He grinned at her as he swiveled in his chair. "My God, isn't that enough?"

She left the office, sensing a full day ahead of her. She was tired from having next to no sleep last night but with several tasks lined up neatly before her, she was able to find the energy. She'd start with the Lentz parents, as she always found speaking to grieving parents one of the most emotionally draining parts of her job.

On her way out, she nearly went to the back of the building where the interrogation rooms were so she could fill Ramirez in on where she would be for the next couple of hours. But they had talked several times about drawing lines between their professional and personal lives. She didn't want it to seem like she was checking in with him, especially not around Finley or any of the other officers.

She exited out of the back of the building and got back behind the wheel of her car. She checked her email and saw that Connelly had sent the address of the Lentzes' friends' house. A little shudder passed through her when she realized that it was on the far side of town, in the direction of Cambridge—where their daughter's body had been found.

60

As she read the address, she got a text message. She saw Rose's name and all of the anxiousness of visiting the Lentz family diminished. She swiped the text up and read it.

Hey. Bad morning. Ugh. Could use some non-judgmental advice and coffee. You busy?

Avery's fingers acted as if controlled by ghosts of the past. She was ready to type: *Sorry, but I'm busy. Maybe this evening?*

But she was done with that. She was learning to prioritize her life, putting Rose first. Yes, she had a job to do, but forty-five minutes over coffee with her daughter was not going to change anything with this case. More than that, it would give the Lentz parents more time to grieve, perhaps putting them in a better state of mind for when Avery finally showed up.

Feeling just a tiny stab of guilt, Avery responded back. *Caffe Nero. 10:00.*

She rolled out of the back lot and out into the streets. She passed a few news vans, wondering what sorts of stories they were trying to drum up about Sophie Lentz. And at the thought of Sophie, a beautiful nineteen-year-old college student, Avery's thoughts then turned to Rose.

What happened to Sophie Lentz…that could have been Rose.

And that was enough to demolish the vestiges of guilt that poked at her for temporarily abandoning her orders. She drove out toward their coffee shop of choice, happy to actually feel like a mother again for the first time in a while.

CHAPTER FIFTEEN

Rose was already sitting at a table with a cup of coffee when Avery arrived at Caffe Nero. When Rose looked up at her, Avery saw that there was a mixture of pain and embarrassment in her face. But there was also a flicker of relief.

Avery sat down, once again realizing that she still felt a little out of place in places like this. Or maybe it wasn't the place or the environment; maybe it was the feeling of knowing that her daughter was actually seeking her guidance.

"How's it going?" Avery asked.

"Been better," Rose said. She was nervously turning her phone over and over again in her hands. It was a nervous tick that Avery had, too. The realization made her smile.

"Want to tell me about it?"

"Sure," Rose said. "That's why I texted you. But…look, Mom. This is huge. The fact that you showed up. You *actually* showed up when I needed you. I got here five minutes ago—a little early, I know—and was sure that you were going to stand me up."

"I won't lie," Avery said. "I've got a pretty terrible case on my mind and I'm all over the place with it right now. But things are going to change, Rose. I know I keep saying things like that, but this time it's going to stick. You're the top priority now."

Rose nodded and Avery could tell that she was trying to fight back tears. She let out a shaky sigh and drummed her fingers on the table as if to distract herself from crying. "Anyway," she said. "So Marcus and I are done. And even though I've been telling myself that he doesn't really mean that much to me, it turns out that he apparently does. Mom…I'm not proud of it but I begged him to stay."

"Stay?" Avery asked, finding the use of that word a little peculiar.

Rose winced, sensing that she had been caught. "He's been staying over a lot," she admitted.

Avery didn't say anything. She had assumed as much. She also knew that Rose was on the pill and was, for the most part, very responsible. "Why did he leave?" she asked.

"I think he sensed things were starting to get serious. He got scared. Or something like that. He was just in it to have fun and—"

She stopped again, sensing one more time that her choice of words had revealed too much. Avery did her best to stay composed, looking beyond the fact that her daughter had basically just told her

62

that the boy she had been seeing was only with her in order to have a sexual relationship with no strings.

"But he was civil about it?" Avery asked.

"I don't know about that," Rose said. "He called me some names. Nothing too bad, though. He was mad…scared. I get it."

"But he wasn't rough with you?" Avery asked.

"No. He never has been. It was just so sudden. And at the risk of sounding conceited, I've always been the one to end relationships. I've never been the one to inflict the pain, you know?"

Avery gave her daughter a thin smile and said, "I feel like I may not have known about most of these relationships."

"Yeah, not so much."

Avery ordered a coffee and sat with Rose, taking her time and enjoying her daughter's company. Avery sipped on her coffee thoughtfully. There was something on her mind, something she had been wanting to tell Rose for a very long time. As the words started to form, she found she was a little nervous about telling it.

"You know, I was usually the one to end relationships, too," she said. "I never really thought about it until just now because really, your father was the first real relationship I ever had. And even in that one, I was selfish."

"Really?" Rose said. "I always assumed Dad was the one that was bossy."

"Oh, he could be. But when my career started to take off, I made it very clear that he was not going to get in my way. We never talked about divorce, not once. Not until the one time…and even then it was a short conversation. We both agreed and that was that. I think that's why we're still *mostly* civil these days."

"So you'd say you were the driving force behind the marriage not working?" Rose asked.

It was a tough question, but the answer was easy.

"For the most part," she said.

"Have you ever admitted it to Dad?"

"Yes. Pretty much right away. At the time, though…I just didn't feel like fighting for our marriage. I don't think he did, either. I'd worn him down over the years."

Rose chuckled nervously and shook her head.

"Damn, Mom. When you open up, you don't hold back, do you?"

"No, I don't."

"So *that's* where I get it from."

As was the case with most of their recent get-togethers, they were eventually laughing through most of the conversation. Two cups of coffee later, after the conversation had finally managed to settle down into less controversial territory, Avery realized that the morning was slipping away and it was almost noon. Rose caught her checking her watch and downed the last bit of her coffee.

"Time to head back to work?" Rose asked.

"Yes, I'd better," she said. "There's quite a bit going on with me...part of which includes a promotion to sergeant. So I need to be on my toes."

"Mom, if you didn't have time to come out here to meet me, you could have just told me."

"No, it was no problem. I need to learn to make time. If this case were blown wide open and we were hot on the trail of a suspect, it would be different. But it's not. When I leave here, I get to go talk to some very sad parents."

"Oh," Rose said as they went to the register. Avery paid for their coffees and they headed back outside. Just as they reached out to hug one another, Avery's phone rang. She checked the display and saw that it was Connelly.

"I have to take this," Avery said.

"That's fine," Rose said. "Thanks for coming out, Mom. I really appreciate it."

"Sure thing," she said.

She then answered the phone and didn't even have time to say *Hello* before Connelly's voice was in her ear. "Black, I need you to wrap up with the Lentzes and come back to the station right now. Things are getting worse with this case."

"I'm not with the Lentzes," she said. "I had a personal matter come up and—"

"You'd damn well better be joking with me," he said.

"No sir. I was with my daughter."

"What the actual fuck, Black?" She could hear him breathing very heavily on the other end of the phone. She did not fear him or any repercussions he might throw her way so she simply let him sort things out without interrupting. "Listen to me and listen closely," he finally said. "I want you back here at the A1 in fifteen minutes. And after you've been debriefed on new events in this case, you and I are having some words in my office."

"New events?" she asked.

"Another letter," Connelly said. "So get back here right now before I change my mind and kick your ass off this case."

CHAPTER SIXTEEN

Avery noticed the media presence even before she reached the station. News vans were swerving through traffic as if the rules of the road did not apply to them. If there had been any cops worth a damn out and about, every one of those vans would easily get at least two tickets each. But Avery drove just as aggressively, though. When she finally pulled into the station lot, some of the vans and crews were already there, setting up in front of the building.

Vultures, Avery thought. *The killer apparently emailed this one out to the media just like the last one.*

She did her best to ignore them as she walked into the station. She heard raised voices from the back of the building, one of which could easily be identified as O'Malley's. Connelly's was buried in there, too. Avery noticed at once that people were speaking in hushed tones and casting her sympathetic glances. Apparently, her name had been dragged through the mud over the last hour or so.

She didn't let it bother her, though. When she approached Connelly's office, she did so without guilt or fear. She also didn't bother knocking, as his door was already open. O'Malley, Finley, and Amy from Forensics were crammed into his office. Poor Amy was standing with her back pressed against the wall, as if she was legitimately afraid of Connelly's temper.

"Black, close the door behind you," Connelly said. He was obviously pissed but had apparently cooled down a bit from when he had called her on the phone.

He picked up a piece of paper from his desk, got to his feet, and stretched across his desk to hand it to her. It was covered in a protective plastic sheet, a feature that keyed her in to what it was before she even saw the paper.

The new letter, she thought as her eyes started to scan it. The entire office fell into silence as she stood there and read it. It was shorter than the last letter but no less sinister. She read it slowly, savoring each word:

Frozen beauty. It melts away longtime scars.
I will keep doing this until I can make the hearts beat again.
I hope you find me. I have so much to show, so much to share.
Oh, this distorted smile.
Oh, this ice in my blood that wants to be thawed.
This winter sprawl is endless even when the warm weather reigns.

The scars won't go away and neither does their beauty—one of God's cruel tricks.

Slowly, Avery handed the letter back to Connelly. He didn't jerk it from her fingers but he did snatch it roughly away. "Any idea just what in the hell that means?"

"Not straightaway, no," she said. "The *I hope you find me* line scares me, though."

"And why is that?" Connelly asked.

"Because he *wants* us to find him. And that means he has no real concept of danger or consequences. It's sort of the same with the line *I have so much to show, so much to share.* I hate to say it, but that indicates that these two bodies might not be the only ones. It makes you wonder…what is it that he wants to show us?"

Connelly was breathing heavily, staring at the letter and making fists out of his hands, clenching and unclenching. He looked around the room slowly and something in his expression made Avery realize that he was having to put forth a lot of effort to remain cool and calm.

"Could you all please give Avery and I a moment alone?" he asked the others in attendance.

Finley, Amy, and O'Malley stepped out of the room quickly. She noticed that Finley looked back at her almost apologetically.

When the door was closed, Avery sat down in the chair in front of his desk. She expected him to scream at any moment but when he spoke, his voice was surprisingly calm. Still, she could sense an undercurrent of rage in it.

"Have you spoken with Ramirez?" he asked. "Do you have any idea where he is?"

"No, I don't."

"Well, because you decided to shirk your duties and apparently do whatever the hell you wanted, he's out speaking with the Lentz parents. He picked up your slack. Now…you want to tell me what you were thinking this morning?"

"Quite frankly, I was thinking my daughter needed me. And since this case is at a standstill, I didn't think spending an hour and a half with my daughter would slow things down.""And you didn't consider that the Lentzes might have been a source of valuable information?"

"Of course I did," Avery said, starting to get a little angry. "But I also know that Sophie Lentz was nineteen when she was killed. The same age as my daughter. So you know what…in the moment, I felt spending time with my daughter took priority. She needed me…and that doesn't happen very often. Besides…you know as well as I do that the Lentzes wouldn't have provided any information. They've been in New York while their daughter was in college. It's not like they were close."

Connelly reclined back in his seat and sighed. "Look…in this situation there's been no real harm done. I have three kids. Did you know that? Two in college and one about to graduate high school. I get it. I do. But these rash spur of the moment decisions have to stop if you're serious about being sergeant. Hell, you could have at least called and told us what was going on."

She wasn't going to apologize; she was sure that wasn't what Connelly was looking for anyway. He just wanted to know that she had heard what he was saying. "Understood," she said. "Now…this letter…I assume it was also sent to the media like the last one?"

"Oh yeah. It's getting bad. Two letters…two bodies. He's making us look like idiots."

"Still nothing from Forensics on the old letter?"

"Nothing," he answered. "I have them looking over the envelope this one came in right now. I'll send the letter down when we're done here."

Avery reached down for the letter again just as someone knocked at the door. When it opened, Ramirez poked his head in. "Is it safe?" he joked.

"Just get in here," Connelly said. "Were the Lentzes any help?"

"Very little," Ramirez said. "The mother was an absolute wreck. There was a strained relationship, but that was back in Arizona. I hate to say it, but the parents are a dead end. They seemed a little ashamed that they didn't know anything about their daughter after she moved off to college, even though they moved to the East Coast right along with her."

"So back to square one," Connelly said. "Can I trust the two of you to get out there and try to pull *something* together?"

Ramirez and Avery shared a look and then a determined nod. "I'll start by just clearing my head," Avery said. "Go back over the case files, maybe revisit the reservoir."

"Why not the dam at Watertown?"

"Because Patty Dearborne floated down the Charles from somewhere else. That was just the site her body was found, not a legit crime scene."

Connelly nodded his understanding. "Fine. Get to work then. And please keep me posted on the hour, every hour. I'd really like to have something to tell these media assholes by the end of the day just to shut them up."

Without another word, Avery and Ramirez walked out of Connelly's office. When the door was closed and they started down the hallway, Avery reached out and gave his hand a little squeeze.

"Thanks for covering for me with the Lentz family."

"No problem. I just wish you would have called. I thought his head was going to explode when he found out you weren't with the Lentzes. Where were you anyway?"

"With Rose."

"She okay?"

"Yes, she's fine. But for now, let's focus on the case, okay?"

"Sure," he said, clearly a little hurt.

"I need some time alone," she said, not being totally honest. "I need to get my head wrapped around this guy and his motives. When I'm done do you want to maybe drive back down to the Fresh Pond Reservoir?"

"Sounds like a plan."

With that, they parted ways. Ramirez headed for his office while Avery made her way toward the elevators. This killer was turning out to be just like the ice that seemed to have such a hold on him—cold and slippery. If she had any hope of getting into his mind and figuring out who he was and why he was acting out, she was going to need some help.

Avery hated to admit it, but she was at a total loss for the first time in her career

And she knew just who she needed to see: Sloane Miller, the A1 psychiatrist.

CHAPTER SEVENTEEN

From time to time, Avery felt guilty for using Sloane's services. Dr. Sloane Miller was on staff to work with officers who were buckling under the pressure and stress of their jobs. Of course, in the A1, most of those officers would never admit they needed help. That's why Avery had never had much of a problem getting a few minutes of Sloane's time.

This afternoon was no different. When Avery entered Sloane's office, she was sitting behind her desk drinking coffee and reading something on her laptop. She gave a genuine smile when she saw Avery step in.

"At the risk of seeming a little too full of myself," Sloane said, "I was thinking I might see you in the next day or so."

"How so?" Avery asked.

"The way the news is talking about these letters we've been getting. The person who wrote those things is *begging* for a psych evaluation. And assuming the guilty party won't just show up at my door, I thought you might."

"Am I that predictable?"

"Predictable isn't the word. I think you're looking for *thorough*."

Avery took a seat on the other side of Sloane's desk. It was much more comfortable than the chair in Connelly's office. "I just can't figure out the sort of man that would do this," Avery said, getting right to the point. "The killing part, sure. Been there, done that. But the inclusion of ice, the absolute neatness of the bodies…it's an equation that just doesn't seem to add up. There are too many pieces that don't complement one another."

"And that's strange to you?" Sloan asked.

"Yes. There's no concrete motive that I can see."

"Well, all of those pieces that don't fit are a clue in and of themselves, I think," Sloane said. "I think your intelligence is getting in the way here. You're trying to make sense of something that has no trace of logic. Based on the bit I know about the case and the nature of these letters, I think a logical approach is going to hinder you."

"Abstract thinking isn't my strong suit," Avery said.

"Oh, I know. But from what I'm seeing, there's some legitimate form of psychological disturbance with this person. The letters themselves denote that they want to be caught, right?"

"I believe so," Avery said. "The latest letter actually says it."

69

"But the fact that the killer is being so careful with what he's doing suggests a need to remain hidden. But why would you want to stay hidden but *hope* someone catches you?"

Avery chewed on this for a moment, the meaning of Sloane's riddle slowly coming together. "It's a cry for help that they don't even know they are making," she said, forming the idea as she spoke it aloud. "He's staying hidden and being careful not to get caught for some subconscious reason—shame, guilt, or something like that. But he wants to be caught because…well, he either wants to brag about what he's doing or he realizes deep down that he needs to be stopped but doesn't have the willpower to stop himself."

And if he wants us to catch him for some subconscious reason, she thought, *that clearly denotes a psychological lapse of some kind. He's kidnapping and killing while, at the same time, knowing it's wrong and wanting to be caught—maybe even realizing he deserves the punishment.*

"Exactly," Sloane said. "So what sort of person might wrestle with such things?"

"Several kinds," Avery said. She smirked, realizing that just like that, Sloan had managed to put her on the right track—a track she had been unable to see due to her logical approach. "But at the root of it all is a reason to stay hidden…something he's ashamed of or hates about himself. And that might mean he has a previous record of some kind. But…there's still too many X-factors."

"Self-loathing and hate could be a very good reason for making sure the bodies are in pristine condition," Sloane suggested. "It could suggest regret or even a battle within his conscience."

Avery nodded. These were all points she had come to on her own and shared with others but to hear them reworded in a more logical way was always helpful.

"I agree," Avery said. "But locating a man driven by self-hatred is like finding a needle in a haystack. There are so many of them. I think the thing that will make this guy stand out is that there seems to be a sort of artistic gesture to it. It's not just that the bodies are hairless and cleaned. I mean, their nails are done, for God's sake."

"Maybe a man who has some sort of sexual identity crisis?"

"Maybe," Avery said. This thought had not occurred to her before. *Makes sense,* she thought. *A man who adores the appearance of women, maybe even envies their bodies…what better way to shave like a woman, to do nails like a woman? It would be*

70

much easier to have the real thing. Maybe this is some sort of fantasy of his, just not of a physically sexual nature.

"No real profile seems to fit just yet," Avery said. "It's still all coming down to finding proper leads."

"Well, once you reach that part of the case, I'm of no use any longer. I believe that's where your skills come in."

Avery let out a little laugh. "You know…I'm taking the role of sergeant sometime in the next month or so. If I have my way, you'll be given much more credit for the work you do."

"Sergeant, huh? That's great news."

"It's also hush-hush for another few weeks, so let's flex that doctor-patient confidentiality thing, why don't we?"

"My lips are sealed," Sloane said. "Now get out of here and catch us a bad guy. If I have to see another one of those desperate letters come across the news, I might scream."

***

Motivated by Sloane's help, Avery headed back to her office. She shut the door and promptly buried her head in the case files. Even with the minor breakthrough she'd had in Sloane's office, Avery was fairly certain that she'd squeezed every drop of available information from the case files. But she thought there might be easy links to information that she'd already read, links that she could find based on her new approach.

Excited by a new direction to take, she slipped into the flow easily, bringing each piece of the puzzle together and shifting the pieces.

Shame and guilt…and some sort of obsession with the cold. Has he committed some previous heinous acts in the cold?

No jewelry…not a matter of theft, though; he just wants the women to be spotless. This is further proven by his ignorant attempt at trying to scrub away the tattoo on Sophie Lentz's back.

Two college girls so far. Was that planned or a coincidence? Different colleges, bodies found twenty-six miles apart. But the Charles River carried Patty Dearborne an unknown distance.

Homemade chloroform. So while there might be a mental break of some sort at play, he's smart enough to do research and make his own chloroform.

Ice…freezing…possible criminal history…

She looked at the sheet for the notes on the Fresh Pond Reservoir and studied it again. *Very few security cameras and they are all at the entrance. According to reports, only two potential*

71

crimes on the premises within the last fifteen years—one a public indecency charge for a couple having sex and another for a hunter that was trespassing.

She thought about this hunter for a minute. According to reports, he was arrested for trespassing. *Arrested? Seems a little severe...*

With the wheels really rolling now, Avery opened up the A1's internal database on her laptop. A few quick keywords and then typing in the address of the Fresh Pond Reservoir pulled up the two items in the report. Completely skipping over the indecent exposure item, she opened up the report on the hunter who had been caught trespassing. She read it slowly, sensing right away that their might be something there.

Jimmy Daughtry, 54, was caught trespassing on the reservoir grounds in November 2015. Had his hunter's license on him, claimed he had no idea he was on private state grounds. Cops were called when shots were fired on the grounds while Daughtry was hunting deer. Became violent with one of the arresting officers when the conversation got heated. Arrested for assault and opening fire on public grounds. Released on $7,500 bail. It was later discovered he had been hunting on the grounds for over two years. Past record of child endangerment and attempted sexual assault of a minor.

Avery then pulled up Jimmy Daughtry's criminal record. The child endangerment had been for his own child; when she was eight, Daughtry had forced his daughter to swim in the Charles River when it was below freezing outside, a form of punishment for her accidentally leaving the front door of their house cracked open in the winter. The attempted sexual assault had occurred in 2007 when Daughtry made advances on a fifteen-year-old girl outside of a convenience store.

She took note of his current address and employer, plugging them both in to her phone's GPS. She then paged Ramirez from her desk phone and found that hearing his voice even at work centered her in an unexpected away.

"You busy?" she asked.

"I wish," he said. "This case is kicking my ass. You?"

"My ass is getting kicked, too," she said. "But how do you feel about taking a ride with me to check on a potential lead?"

"I'll meet you at the car."

And just like that, the case started to seem a bit more promising and Avery started to feel that familiar surge of hope and adrenaline.

72

CHAPTER EIGHTEEN

Rather ironically, Jimmy Daughtry worked at an outdoor sports shop. It was a second-hand family-owned business situated in the rural area that sat just outside of Cambridge. When Avery stepped inside, she was a little overwhelmed. She had been into sports stores before, sure, but never one where hunting and fishing were the main draws.

Clothing racks were packed with camo suits and insulated jackets, most of which were bright orange. The entire rear wall was paneled in glass casing, containing a variety of guns. While most of them were basic hunting rifles, a few might have drawn the suspicion of someone working with the ATF.

Fishing rods and reels were on the wall to the right while other assorted hunting equipment lined the shelves of the opposite wall— everything from duck calls to concentrated bottles of deer urine.

She approached the counter in the back, situated in front of the guns, and found two men at work. One was working with a customer, filling out a form for the purchase of a firearm. The other was a man who appeared to be in his fifties, his long gray hair combed back. He was looking through a brochure and placing orders into a computer. It was this man that Avery approached. When she drew near, he looked up from the computer. The look he gave her was at first a comical one—wondering what a prim and proper woman was doing in this sort of place, no doubt. But then he apparently put two and two together after noticing her attire as well as the well-dressed man accompanying her. After that, the look on his face became rather grave.

"Good afternoon," Avery said, putting on her most pleasant voice in order to keep the man calm before the conversation even started. "We're looking for Jimmy Daughtry."

"That's me," he said.

"I'm Detective Avery Black with Boston's A1 Homicide Division. I was hoping to have about five minutes of your time to ask you a few questions."

"What for?" he asked, instantly on the defensive.

"I'd really rather discuss it in private. Is there a break room or something around here?"

"There's a stock room in the back," he said, more angry than he was nervous or afraid. "But I'm going to have to clear it with my boss. Can you give me a second?"

Avery nodded and watched as Daughtry walked over to the man that was still filling out a form for the store's only current customer. The boss looked over his shoulder, rolled his eyes when he saw Avery and Ramirez, and then shrugged.

Daughtry then waved them over. Avery walked to the end of the counter where Daughtry led them to the back of the store and through a small door. They entered a small stock room that was crammed with boxes and catalogues. A stuffed deer head was on one wall and a picture of a large-breasted woman in a bikini on the beach was on the opposite wall.

"Homicide, you say?" Daughtry said. "That's a new one. We get government spooks in here all of the time to make sure we ain't selling illegal guns. And it's been awhile since the law came pestering me about the dumb shit I did years ago. But homicide…yeah, that's new."

"Well, last night there was a body pulled from the Fresh Pond Reservoir," Avery said. "And since that is the same place you were busted for illegally shooting a firearm, you're a candidate for questioning."

"For what?" he asked. "Dumping a body in the reservoir? Hunting on state-owned land and murder are two totally separate crimes. Shouldn't a detective know that?"

"Well, quite frankly," Avery said, ignoring his lame insult, "it's the child endangerment and attempted sexual assault of a minor that makes you more of a suspect. Make no mistake…you are being accused of absolutely nothing. Your name just happens to be connected to the site where the body was found. If you can provide solid alibis, we'll be out of your hair."

"This body…was it like the one you pulled out of the Charles a few nights ago?"

"I'm not at liberty to share case details with you," Avery said. "All I need from you right now is to know where you were last night."

He frowned and looked to the big-breasted woman on the poster, as if she might encourage him. "I was ice fishing."

"Where?"

"On the Charles. I just started doing it this year. It sucks. But it's a good reason to act like a fool on the ice and have a few beers."

"Can anyone verify this?" Ramirez asked.

"Yeah. There were three of us out there. Call my friends Early Wright and Mike Simmons. They'll tell you."

"Did you catch anything?" Avery asked.

"Hell no. We started plugging at the ice like I read online and it started splintering. Earl damn near fell into the river when the ice started breaking."

"I see," Avery said. "Can you give me their addresses?"

"Yeah," Daughtry said, pulling out his phone. "You know…it's none of my business, but if some girl was pulled out of the reservoir and he wasn't caught on camera, there's only one place he could have done it without being seen."

"I assume you know this from your hunting days?" Ramirez asked.

"Yes. There's an old trail that runs along the backside, just where the state property takes over. He had to have gone down that. And not a lot of people know it's there."

"You're certain?" Avery asked.

"Pretty sure," Daughtry said. He then showed Avery his phone where he had pulled up the contacts for his friends. Avery typed them into her phone and saved them.

"Mr. Daughtry, thank you for your assistance. I'm sure you'll understand my closing with asking about your previous offenses."

"You can ask what you want, but I'm not like that anymore. Well…not the child abuse and the thing with the minor. The hunting thing…I still think the state ropes off too much land that should be open to the public. But no…I ain't been trespassing neither."

Just a man trying to escape his demons, Avery thought. She'd seen it a hundred times before. Most of the time she could tell when they were being sincere. She couldn't quite get a gauge on Jimmy Daughtry, though. She assumed this unexpected visit from someone from the Homicide division would scare any last temptation out of him.

They left the shop, Ramirez taking an admiring look at some of the fishing rods on his way out.

"You fish?" she asked as they walked out the door.

"I used to. My old man loved it. I tried to carry on the tradition for a while after he passed, but it didn't stick."

There's still so much I don't know about this man, she thought. An alarming thought, given that they'd be living together soon.

"Speaking of which," Ramirez said, "you asked Daughtry if he caught anything when he tried ice fishing. I know you don't care if he caught anything or not. What was the point of that?"

"The ice out on the Charles River was strong enough to skate on, but it was still pretty thin from what I could see. I had a relative that used to be into fishing, too. Ice fishing, in Alaska. That's how I

75

knew that the ice anywhere near here would basically chip away and dump him in the river. That, plus he's not likely to catch anything in this area while ice fishing."

"Ah, so you were trying to catch him in a lie," Ramirez said.

"Exactly."

"You ever do that weird voodoo conversation crap on me, trying to trip me up?"

"Wouldn't you like to know?" she said as she got in the car.

She was trying her best to lift the mood because she knew in the back of her head that if Jimmy Daughtry's alibis turned out to back him up, they were back to having no leads at all.

CHAPTER NINETEEN

The water pipes had frozen and he knew if he wasn't careful, one could burst and make one hell of a mess. But honestly, that sort of mess was the farthest thing from his mind. The thermostat read thirty degrees, as he had cut the heat off yesterday morning (not that it really mattered, as he never set the heat above fifty-five no matter how cold it was outside). He was shivering although he was dressed in sweats and a hooded sweatshirt with a blanket draped over his shoulders and pulled tightly over him.

The apartment was freezing, which was good. He wanted to get himself used to the cold but knew he needed to do it slowly. He had already attempted one experiment last night, standing out in the cold, directly in a puddle of shallow water behind his apartment complex. He'd worn no shoes and this morning one of his toes was discolored and partially numb.

He was moments away from another experiment. He eyed his materials on the kitchen table. The days of freezing hamsters and trying to bring them back to life were over. He had not been thinking clearly back then. He was not trying to resurrect the dead, after all. He was not trying to thaw frozen hearts in the hopes of understanding how to manipulate the effects of the cold—although that *had* been his plan at first. No…he knew better now.

Now he knew he had to *use* the cold. He had to accept it for what it was. He was pretty sure he would no longer be able to capture the beauty of his victims. It might be possible, but minds such as his were not capable of such understanding. If he wanted to truly capture the beauty he saw in those frozen girls, he needed to be one with the cold. If he planned to one day reconfigure himself, to do away with the scarring and the horrible state of his face, he was going to have to embrace the cold. He'd have to love it. To become one with it. And *then* perhaps he could claim the frozen beauty of him victims for himself.

As he sat down at the table, a moan of anticipation escaped his lips. He looked to the Yeti cooler on the table and slowly pried the lid off. Cold vapor rose up from it. He peered inside, eyeing the dry ice with equal amounts of longing and fear.

He rolled up the sleeve of his sweatshirt, realizing that he was beginning to breathe heavily. *I can do this,* he thought. *I can do this. Embrace the cold…be the cold…this is for your face, for your life…*

He placed his hand into the cooler. The cold was a shock at first but after several seconds, his flesh almost felt as if it was

77

getting accustomed to it. He knew there would be a burning sensation but when it came, it was a bit harsher than he had expected.

He'd read up on dry ice a while back and knew that it could be very effective for his experiments and for the ultimate plan. He had used it twice already, preserving the victims. Of course, that was back when he had hoped to resurrect them, to understand how to cheat death with the use of ice.

He knew that you were supposed to use insulated gloves when handling dry ice. He also knew that it was much colder than normal ice, boasting an average temperature of -109.3 degrees Fahrenheit.

Every muscle in his body begged for him to withdraw his hand. But he pushed through it, letting out a little hiss of pain through his teeth. When it got to its absolute worst, he picked up the mirror he had placed by the cooler. He looked at his reflection, staring at the scarring and his drooping mouth. He could still see traces of the man he had once been, a ghost of how he had once looked.

He could be beautiful again if he could just make it through the pain. He had known from the start that it was not going to be easy.

The burn continued. From what he had read, it took a while to pass. It would be replaced by numbness. After that, there could be nerve damage or complete uselessness of the digits. His body was shaking now. How long had his hand been in there? Six minutes? Seven?

Slowly, he withdrew most of his hand from the ice. He left the pinky, though. If he lost that, it would not be that big of a deal. But he'd need the use of his hand. There was important work to do.

Mind over matter, he thought as he started to feel nothing more than a slight twinge of pain and then minor discomfort in the pinky. *You can do this, you can do this.*

"You can do this," he said out loud, speaking to the image in the mirror. "You can do this…"

Out of nowhere, another surge of pain rocketed through his pinky and catapulted into his hand and up his arm. The burning sensation was back tenfold and it came on so strongly that he could not help himself. He withdrew his hand and held it to his chest. He was crying now, choking back a scream because he had to be strong.

He slammed the mirror against the table in frustration. *How can you be so damned weak?*

The mirror shattered. Glass rained down to the floor but he barely even registered it. He looked at his left hand, the one that had been submerged in dry ice for roughly eleven minutes. The pinky

78

had gone a deep shade of purple and the top portion of his ring finger was just a shade lighter. He attempted to move both fingers and found that the pinky was mostly unresponsive. He could feel it wanting to move more, but it was not obeying.

Forget about this, something in his head said. It was a familiar voice, but one he did not like to hear...the voice of his mother. *Oh, honey...forget about this. Turn the heat back on. See a doctor about your hand and that toe. Get out of this while you can. Don't be a moron. Don't fuck this up, too.*

"No," he moaned. "It's too late."

Besides, what did his mother know about anything? It was his mother who had put him in this situation. His mother had driven him to this.

He looked down to the shards of broken glass on the floor almost lovingly. He could pick one up and slide it hard against his jugular. He could do that and it would be easy. He would bleed out quickly. It would all be over.

It was tempting. But he had come this far. He had taken life. To take his own life at this point would be counterproductive.

He looked down at the fingers of his left hand again. Trembling, he let out a shriek. He stormed out of the kitchen and grabbed his keys from the little board by the front door. By the time he reached his van, most of the feeling had come back in his left hand. As far as he was concerned, the pins and needles sensation he felt as the blood resumed its normal business beneath his skin was encouragement enough to carry on with his original plans.

And that's what he was going to do...his mother's ghostlike voice be damned.

***

He already knew who he wanted. He'd seen her several times before. She was a bit older than he was looking for but her beauty could not be denied. He had been watching this woman for seven months now, waiting and planning. He drove around the block for a while, making sure the woman's car was parked where it usually was.

He started to feel almost like a robot. Whenever he was so close to taking them, his mind seemed to slip into automatic mode. Everything was simple and fluid. Everything moved like it was on a track. He felt it and accepted it. He was no longer worried that he could still not feel anything in his left pinky. The only thing important now was getting the woman.

79

He knew the woman lived alone. He'd studied and planned, as he had with the other two. He did not believe in chances or coincidences. It all had to be planned. He'd been working on this for two years now, waiting for this, the coldest winter in the last ten years.

He parked four cars behind the woman's vehicle and watched as she came out of a four-story office building and got in her expensive sleek black car. When the woman pulled into traffic, he followed.

The drive home usually took twenty-one minutes but it took twenty-eight this afternoon because some idiot had run a red light and T-boned a dump truck. He nearly lost sight of the woman in the directed traffic around the accident but caught up to her two blocks from her house. He stayed two cars behind her the entire way, not wanting to be seen.

When the woman parked at her home, pulling into her garage, she never noticed the red van passing by and turning left at the block.

He went around the block, going through the woman's routine in her head. In fifteen minutes or so, she'd come outside with her dog—one of those weird cutesy half-poodle breeds. That gave him plenty of time. He circled the block and parked behind the woman's car. She never came out of the front door to walk her dog, so she wouldn't see the red van parked behind her.

Very carefully, he took the small squeeze bottle out of his coat pocket, along with the dishrag. He made sure to hold his breath as he soaked the cloth in the chloroform. When he had applied just a little but more than enough, he got out of the van and started across the woman's lawn as if he belonged there. His hands were stuffed in his pockets, his right hand loosely holding the cloth.

He'd scoped out the house before. He knew there was a perfect hiding spot just by the stairs along the back porch. He remained close to the house, hugging the side, just in case the woman decided to randomly look out of the window. When he reached the back porch, he hunkered down by the back steps, pressing his back against the latticework along the back of the porch.

The machine-like feeling of working under a system that was out of his control allowed him to be patient and perfectly still. His legs were bent so he could spring up quickly when he needed to. His breathing was thin and slow. He was the picture of patience, waiting, understanding what was at stake here.

Four minutes later, the back door opened. He could hear the clicking of the dog's paws as the woman led it to the back porch.

There was a notable change to the sound as the dog stepped off of the kitchen's linoleum and onto the wooden back porch. The woman, he knew, would have her earbuds in, listening to her iPod (a blue one, he had seen as he had passed her on the street several times).

When he heard the first footfall land on the steps, he sprang to his feet. The woman was shocked and scared, freezing for a moment. The dog was terrified too, breaking into a series of pathetic little yelps. He reached out and grabbed the puffy shoulder of the woman's jacket. He slung her to the ground and was on top of her before the woman could let out a scream. When the woman did manage to finally open her mouth to shout, the washcloth was instantly stuffed into it. She made a slight gagging noise and stopped trying to fight at once. Her eyes grew wide with alarm.

Beside her, the dog leaped on its owner's attacker but did no damage. It was swatted away with one hard backhand and then seemed to lose interest, letting out a little bit of urine before cowering under the back porch stairs.

It watched as its owner stopped struggling, her right arm going upward in a failed punch. She then went limp and the man that had attacked her caressed the side of her face in an almost loving way. When the man with the cloth in his hand stood up and struggled to get its owner up on his shoulder, the dog remained hidden under the porch steps, letting out one final little yelp.

CHAPTER TWENTY

Avery had to remind herself several times over the course of the afternoon that the case was, as of right now, out of her hands. Jimmy Daughtry's alibis had indeed panned out, leaving them with zero leads once again. As it stood, the only hope they had was that Forensics could turn up some new piece of evidence.

She hated feeling that she was sitting on the sidelines, but she also knew that it was the perfect opportunity to put her priorities in order once again. She was eventually going to have to learn that it was okay to have a life outside of work—and now with things going smoothly with Rose and her relationship with Ramirez at an almost too-good-to-be-true level, it seemed like a good time.

After leaving the A1 at seven that evening, she and Ramirez swung by his place and picked up a few boxes. They were almost childlike with glee when they stowed them in the back of Avery's car and drove back to her apartment together. It was a particularly special moment for Avery because she knew that Rose would be by later. She had not yet told Rose about the news of Ramirez moving in and was, quite honestly, a little nervous about it. But still...the two of them together was an idea that made her heart swell.

It felt like it might burst when they arrived at the apartment and she saw that Rose was already there. She was waiting in her car, unable to be buzzed in. She got out and greeted them as they approached the front steps. Ramirez was carrying two boxes stacked on top of one another and Avery was rolling a suitcase along behind her.

"Hey, guys," Rose said with a knowing smile on her face and tone to her voice. "So...what's going?"

"Come on upstairs," Avery said. "We'll talk about it."

"OK..." Rose said.

Something in her daughter's eyes gave her away, though. Avery could tell that Rose had figured it out before they even reached the elevator. Rather than let it hang in the air and cause unnecessary tension, Avery grinned and said: "What do you think of this?"

Rose looked to Ramirez and gave him a surprised look. "So you're moving in?"

He nodded. "Yes. But if it makes you feel weird for any reason, we can talk about it."

My God, Avery thought, her heart fit to burst. *He actually means it.*

82

"No, I think it's awesome," Rose said. "It means I can stop worrying about her because there will be at least one responsible adult in her apartment."

"Damn," Ramirez said. "You just got burned, babe."

"Yeah…she's sort of like her mom in that respect."

"Ah hell," he said. "I'm in for some trouble living here, aren't I? Both of you around all the time…"

"We'll take it easy on you," Avery said.

"At first," Rose added.

By the time the elevator doors dinged open and they stepped on with the boxes, all three of them were laughing. It made Avery feel warm…*safe*. Something about this felt right, as if someone had been hiding the last piece of some huge puzzle and had just discovered it and snapped it into place.

***

After a few slices of pizza were downed and Ramirez had slid his boxes into a corner in the bedroom, Rose brought up a question that Avery and Ramirez had somehow managed to dodge. She meant no harm by it—Avery knew that right away—but it was still a rather abrupt question.

"So, if I may be so bold," Rose said with a smile, "can I ask what this means? Moving in together is a *step*. Are there more steps ahead?"

Avery and Ramirez shared a startled glance but they both smiled. "I think that's a conversation we need to have together before we can discuss it with anyone else," Avery said.

"Mom, let's face it, you're not getting any younger. You better figure this stuff out before it's too late."

Ramirez let out a laugh that was a little too genuine for Avery's taste. She nudged him in the side and rolled her eyes. "You're no spring chicken, either," she reminded him.

"It's cool, though," Rose said. "I'm happy for you, Mom. I really am."

It did Avery a world of good to hear that from Rose. Less than a year ago Rose had been badgering her to get back together with Rose's father—to at least give him a chance. Avery wondered where the change of heart had come from. It occurred to her then that in all of the attempts to become a better mother and to make sure she was a permanent fixture in Avery's life, they had not discussed Tom, her father, much at all.

The night wound down and as ten o'clock approached, Rose made her way to the front door. "This has been fun," she announced, "but the third wheel is now leaving. I'll be happy to come help unpack when everything else is here, though."

"Honey, you're not a third wheel," Avery said.

"She's right," Ramirez said. "If anything, *I'm* the third wheel."

Rose smiled and shook her head. "No sir. Bedtime is soon. Who do you think Mom would prefer be here when the lights go out? You or me?"

"Rose!" Avery said, embarrassed and a little shocked.

"Whatever, Mom," Rose laughed. "It's okay. You get yours."

Avery did not embarrass very easily but she felt heat flushing her face. "Goodnight, Rose," she said, shaking her head in disbelief.

"G'night, lovebirds," Rose said and made her exit.

When the door closed behind her, Ramirez said, "That girl's got spunk."

"I know. And the better she and I reconnect, the more I'm seeing. I'd like to say she gets it from her father but I think you and I both know that's not the case."

"That's for sure," Ramirez said. He was in the kitchen, straightening up the pizza boxes and dishes from dinner. "She's smart, too. Wicked smart."

Avery nodded. "I still feel like I've missed so much of her life."

"Well, let's be honest," Ramirez said. "You did. And that sucks. But you've made it right. You're here for her now. And you can tell she appreciates it."

She joined him in the kitchen and approached him from behind. She wrapped her arms around his waist and rested her head on his back, just between his shoulders. "Thanks," she said.

"You okay?" he asked her.

"I am," she said. "And you know, she *is* smart. She knew when to leave. Maybe she could sense it in the air."

"Sense what?"

Still holding him from behind, Avery slowly slid her hand down to the button of his pants and unclasped it. "That her mother wanted to be alone with her roommate. Or, as she put it, that her mother wanted to *get hers*."

"Told you," Ramirez said, turning to face her with a devilish smile on his face. "Smart girl."

***

84

Afterwards, they sat on the kitchen floor, their backs pressed against the cabinets. Their clothes were in a pile on the floor beside them. The whole scenario made Avery feel about twenty years younger, like one of those excited couples that had made a pact to have sex in every room of the house.

Maybe not a bad idea, she thought.

"I think I'm going to like living with you," Ramirez said with a smile, a little out of breath. He leaned over and kissed her bare shoulder.

"Likewise," she said.

"I do feel like there's something I should share with you, though," he said.

"What's that?"

"Well, I haven't been married, but I came really close one time. I know you and I have never really had that conversation. And if this is going to stick, I think it's a part of my past that you need to know about."

"Okay," she said.

"I met her in college, freshman year. From the first date, she was it for me. No sleeping around in college like guys are supposed to do. Four years in college, two after college, most of which was me in the academy. I bought a ring and everything. I was just getting up the nerve, you know? I had that damn thing for six weeks and just couldn't bring myself to do it. And it was a good thing, too. I came home early one day to surprise her. Had the ring on me, thinking I might pop the question after a really nice dinner."

Avery tried her hardest but could not envision Ramirez getting down on one knee. *Too much vulnerability,* she thought. *He must have been a very different person back then.*

"I think I see where this is going," Avery said. "And you don't have to finish it if you don't want to."

"Eh, it's okay," he said. "I haven't actually talked about it out loud for years. It's sort of cathartic, you know?"

"Yeah, I get that," she said, fully realizing that she had not yet shared her history with her previous marriage. *That's got to happen soon. Can't keep dodging it forever...especially since he's now living with me.*

"So I roll up to the apartment, a little nervous because maybe this is the night, you know? And...man, I can hear it before I see it. And you'd think hearing it would make me *not* want to see it, but I *had* to see it. Sounds dumb, huh? Anyway, I walk to the bedroom and realize it's coming from the shower. The bathroom door is open and we had one of those nice glass shower doors. So I saw it all.

85

This dude's bare ass as he's taking her from behind. And she's really enjoying it. Like *really* enjoying it.

"I snapped. I opened the door quietly and the guy didn't even know anything was going on until I grabbed him by the shoulder and wheeled him around. I punched him and when he fell into the shower, I pushed my girlfriend to the side. I got soaked under that water but it was worth it. I won't even lie about it. It took her pulling me off of him to prevent me getting in some very serious trouble. I'm pretty sure I broke his nose. Maybe dislocated his jaw."

"How did she react?" Avery asked.

He shrugged. "No idea. I turned around and left. I haven't spoken to her since."

"Not a single time?" she asked.

He shook his head. "She tried calling me a few times but I never answered. I returned that ring and used the cash for a down payment on a new car. I still have the car, actually." He chuckled at this, but there was no humor in it.

It's a sad story, Avery thought. *But it sure does explain a lot.*

"Thanks for letting me know," she said. "I realize there's a lot of stuff we still don't know about one another. I don't know if that makes this more exciting or sort of cautionary."

"A bit of both, I think," he said.

"God...that has to sting, thinking about it."

"Not really," he said. "It hurts more to know that I could have probably killed that guy if she hadn't pulled me off of him."

"Still. It sucks you had to go through that."

He shrugged and then leaned over and kissed her softly on the mouth. When he drew back, they looked into one another's eyes and God help her, she had butterflies in her stomach.

Maybe now is the time to tell him, she said. *Everything about Tom and how my selfishness and career obsession ruined it all.*

She summoned up the courage and pushed the first words to her tongue.

But she was interrupted right away as her phone started ringing behind them. Feeling a little foolish for still being completely nude in the kitchen, she got up and grabbed it off of the couch.

"It's O'Malley," she said.

"What is it with the bosses calling after sex?" he asked.

"Could be worse," she said. "It could have been *during.*"

She answered the call, sitting on the couch and pulling a blanket around her. "Hey, O'Malley. What is it?"

"A third body," he said. "And this one...Jesus, you just have to see it."

CHAPTER TWENTY ONE

It was just shy of midnight when Avery parked on the street opposite the Boston Public Library, hardly believing where she was—that there could actually be a body in the center of Boston. There were only two other cars on the scene so far, which made Avery think Connelly was trying to keep this new body as quiet as possible. When she and Ramirez got out of the car, it was not the library that interested them, but the little stretch of land on the other side of the street. During most of the winter, this served as something of a makeshift artist's space. As of late, it just so happened that the city was billing it as an ice sculpture park.

She spotted O'Malley and Finley right away. They were speaking with a tall man who looked very upset. They were the only three people in the area at the moment. As she and Ramirez drew closer to the three men, she quickly glanced at the creations around them: ice sculptures of angels, snowmen, swans, even one of the Red Sox mascot with the baseball for a head.

But up ahead was a creation that clearly was not supposed to be there. It was evident in the fact that it was covered by a blanket—the same sort of blanket that was carried around in the trunks of just about every police car in town. O'Malley, Finley, and the tall man were standing in front of it. Whatever the blanket was covering, it was about two and a half feet tall and in a slumped shape.

Avery wasted no time, hurrying over to the three men. "What have we got?" she asked.

"Take a quick look under the sheet and see for yourself," O'Malley said.

Avery did, not sparing a second to prepare herself for the worst. She had long ago learned that when you expected something to be very bad, it almost never met your expectations, therefore making the crime not seem quite as severe.

She drew the blanket back and found a naked woman sitting on the sidewalk. She was extremely pale. Her hair had chunks of ice in it. She was sitting in a modified version of what she had called criss-cross-applesauce in school. The woman's blue eyes were wide open, staring ahead toward the library across the street. It took Avery less than five seconds to see that this woman was hairless, like all the rest. Arms, legs, pubic region, everything except the hair on her head.

And, like the others, the woman was incredibly attractive. One thing was different, though. This woman appeared to be older than the other two girls. Maybe by as much as ten to fifteen years.

Behind the body were two simply constructed stands, two beams sawed and nailed together to support her in the sitting position. An iron bar ran between them, sitting flush with the concrete.

This is it...the proof needed to determine that he sees this as art of some kind, Avery thought. *She may not be covered in ice, but she's been exposed to it—that much is clear from the bits of ice in her hair. And displaying her like this...this is him rubbing our noses in it. No need to send one of his cute letters to the precinct this time. This* is *his letter.*

Having had her look and allowing Ramirez to also study the body, she covered it back up. "How long has she been here?" Avery asked.

It was the tall man who answered. His voice trembled when he spoke. "Not very long. I left here at eight thirty. It was discovered around ten after eleven."

"Detective Black," O'Malley said, "meet Jonathan Hughes. He's a local sculptor who has been overseeing the ice sculpture park. He was the first person we called when we learned about the body. She was discovered by a couple coming home from a bar. They decided to check out the ice sculptures and saw this. There was less than a three-hour window."

"Someone *had* to have seen something," Ramirez said.

"Probably," O'Malley said. "But we got no calls. Just the bar-hopping couple."

"Do we have an ID?" Avery asked.

"We do. And it took Mr. Hughes here to point it out to me. The woman under the blanket is Carolyn Rodgers, vice president of the Boston Historical Society and sometimes-model."

"Sometimes?" Avery asked.

"She's been in commercials, some print ads, a music video for some country music guy. A shitload of people know who she is— which means that this is the body of a public figure. So I would love to get to the bottom of this before the media smells it."

Avery looked around the small ice sculpture park and saw the one thing they had going for them was that the body had not been visible from the street. However, seeing the library across the street gave her an idea. The Old South Church also sat across the street, a gorgeous piece of architecture that sent her mind into motion.

88

"Finley, can you make a call to see who we need to speak with to get access to the security cameras at the library and Old South Church? You're going to piss some people off calling so late, but we need to be looking at footage within the hour."

"I don't see how anyone could have done this without someone noticing something suspicious," Jonathan Hughes said.

Cold weather means big coats and stocking caps, she thought. *That's a built-in disguise right there...*

"It's cold and it's an ice sculpture park," Avery said. "If anyone saw someone walking into here with any sort of package— even if it was big enough to be a human body—I don't know that anyone would have *known* it was suspicious. We'll get more answers if we can get something from the library footage."

"I'm on it," Finley said, taking out his phone.

Avery held in a sigh and turned around to the look at the small area that made up the sculpture garden. At this time of night on a Sunday, it would have been next to impossible for the killer to get a body in here without anyone seeing it.

He's bold. He's courageous in a morbid sort of way. If we don't catch him soon, this could get very nasty.

Sure, the passersby might not know it was a body the killer was carrying—but someone within that three-hour window must have seen *something.* For now, their only hope was finding something on the library security cameras.

Looking around at the beautiful sculptures while in the presence of the body was eerie. Finally letting out her sigh, Avery shuddered.

It was going to be another long night.

***

Forty minutes later, Avery and Ramirez were sitting in a very small office with a middle-aged woman in the Boston Public Library. The woman was Jessie Nelson, head librarian and, apparently, the only one on staff that knew her way around the security system outside of the company that installed it—and they could not get anyone out to meet with Avery until around noon tomorrow.

Jessie was as helpful as she could be, having been pulled out of her sleep shortly after midnight. She was glad to help, though, and showed an attitude of concern as she clicked and scrolled her way through the footage between eight o'clock and eleven fifteen that night.

Right away, Avery noticed one disheartening thing: the security cameras outside of the library were not able to catch all of the scenery across the street. About a quarter of the left side of the sculpture park was cut off. Still, the small plot of sidewalk where Carolyn Rodgers had been displayed was in plain view.

As Avery had expected, the flow of foot traffic tapered off around nine o'clock, then dipped down to virtually nothing by ten.

"Okay," Avery said over Jessie's shoulder. "Now, I want you to please stop and play in real time every time someone comes by the sculpture park between ten o'clock and when Ramirez and I arrive."

"Got it," Jessie said, fast forwarding through the footage. She stopped when two people went walking by at 10:06. The two were clearly a younger couple, walking close and holding hands. They walked by the sculptures without walking through the small park and continued on their way down the street.

A single person walked by at 10:11 and although he walked into the park, he was carrying nothing. Still, Avery had Jessie slow down the footage. They watched the man enter and then presumably exit out of the side that was cut off by the camera.

Another person passed six minutes later, then a group of five that were obviously college students three minutes after that. Jessie continued to scroll, sitting upright and on the edge of her seat.

Then at 10:39, someone stepped into view. They were not trying to be inconspicuous at all. It was a figure wearing a thick coat. The hood was pulled up and as they came into the screen, they were looking down at the street. This could be to either hide their face or because they were putting force into pulling the metal dolly behind them. A large wooden crate was on the dolly, teetering on the edge.

"Holy shit," Ramirez said.

"Go back to where they came in and slow it down, please," Avery said.

Jessie did as she was asked. They watched as the hooded figure very slowly entered the frame, pulling the crate behind them. They entered the sculpture park as if they belonged there, maneuvering through the sculptures and heading directly for an empty spot near the back, where Avery had seen the body of Carolyn Rodgers less than an hour ago.

The figure stopped at that exact spot and unloaded the crate from the dolly. The person took a quick look around and then pried the crate open. As Avery had expected, the body of Carolyn Rodgers was inside. The figure remained with its back to the

90

camera as it brought the morbid sculpture out and set it up on its makeshift stands.

The entire process took about two minutes; in that time, no one else walked by. The figure suddenly stood up, stacking the broken crate in a stack on the dolly. They then walked away from the scene, pulling the dolly behind them as if it was just another normal moment. Like the spectators before the coated and hooded figure, they walked away, exiting to the left and disappearing off of the screen.

"You see a clear shot of the face?" Ramirez asked.

"No. Jessie, can you replay that for us, maybe a bit slower?"

They rewatched the footage and came to only two occasions where the killer's face was pointed at the camera. The first time, the hood and the shadow it cast across their face hid most of it. All that was visible was the lower left side of the killer's face. The second shot was a little more promising but still not great; the fluffy trim of the coat's hood hid most of the killer's face but did manage to reveal one eye, the slope of nose, and everything from the bottom lip down.

"Pause it, please," Avery said. "And can you print that for us?"

Jessie clicked a few commands and said: "Printing now."

She then got up from behind the desk and went to the other side of the office, where a printer was churning the photo out.

"I don't care how crazy you are," Ramirez said. "To drop a body off in a public place like that…that's pretty brazen."

"It is," Avery says. "And it also scares me. If our killer is brave enough to do something like this, I'm not sure there's much he *wouldn't* do."

At that moment, her phone rang. Finley was on the other line and he sounded just as defeated as Avery felt. "Got anything?" Avery asked.

"No," Finley said. "I'm over here at the Old South Church with the security guy. None of their cameras pan around far enough to get a clear shot of the sculpture park. We can see shadows of people when they leave, but just barely. There's nothing of use over here."

"Thanks for trying," Avery said, hanging up and looking back to the screen in front of her. Her concentration was broken when Jessie came back with a printed copy of the man from the footage.

"Thanks," Avery said absently.

She looked to the murky face in the picture. She was slowly overcome with a sense of dread. It was frustrating to know that although this was very likely their killer, the shot did not reveal his face. In that, Avery felt like even from within the picture, the bastard was smiling at her.

CHAPTER TWENTY TWO

Avery had managed to catch a quick nap in one of the A1 break rooms, dozing off and on for about two hours. When she came back out into the melee that was the precinct just prior to 6:30 a.m., the place was a madhouse. The news was all over the television and the press was already setting up camp in the parking lots and street surrounding the building.

Sometime between 2:00 and 6:30 in the morning, the press managed to find out the identity of the latest victim—the body that had been made to look like a sculpture. Because Jonathan Hughes, the overseer and curator of the little park was insisting his innocence, it was assumed that the couple that had discovered the body had leaked it to the press, and probably for a nice sum of money.

The black-and-white photo that she and Ramirez had taken from the library had made the rounds but everyone had a quiet look of disappointment when they saw it. Even when it was enlarged and cleaned up by the experts downstairs in the A1, it was impossible to get any real identity from it. All they had to go on was a dark parka-like coat—probably black. Needless to say, such a feature was beyond common during the winter in Boston.

She made her way quickly to the bathroom, splashed some cold water on her face, and did her best to make some sort of sense out of her hair. She then made a direct line to the coffee maker, poured a mug, and drank it black and hot right away. No sooner had she swallowed the first mouthful than Connelly came toward her as if they were magnetized.

He didn't even bother asking if they could talk in private. He simply cornered her, though not in a hostile way. He spoke quietly and she could tell by the look in his eye that he was tired, too.

"Sorry I wasn't at the ice sculpture park," he said. "Just to let you know, I wasn't there because I was on the phone with the State Police and the feds. There is some serious talk about the FBI getting involved in this. And Jesus, I really don't want that to happen. Level with me, Black. Does this new body provide any further details or insights into this creep?"

"Aside from the fact that he's brave as hell? I'm afraid not. It *does* solidify my theory that this might be some obscure form of art to him, though."

"That doesn't make me feel any better," Connelly said. "Another thing that doesn't make me feel any better is that if the feds do sweep in on this, I'm going to hand it to them without complaint. I'd also pull you off of it."

"What? Why would you do that?"

"Because I don't want my soon-to-be sergeant taking the position on the heels of a case that got the better of her. It would look bad for you and the whole A1."

She wanted to argue but knew he was right. She also knew that the media-related mess involving Carolyn Rodgers pretty much made it a certainty that the FBI would be on the case. Probably within less than a day. If another of those damned letters arrived, it might be even sooner than that.

"One more thing," Connelly said. "Because Carolyn Rodgers was sort of a public figure, the mayor is sticking his fat nose in this. Between you and me, I think he wants to keep the FBI away. So while it's no secret that he's not your biggest fan, he also knows you're the best I've got. Let's try to keep him as happy as possible, okay? But if the topic happens to come up in the near future, let's pretend this conversation wasn't as docile as this. I was supposed to tear into you."

"Mayor's request?"

He nodded sleepily. "This is a mess, Avery. See what you can do about keeping the FBI away from here, huh? Let's wrap it up and get you pushed into that sergeant position with a hell of a win following you in."

Sounds good, she thought as she nodded her agreement. *But this creep is turning out to be just as slick as the ice he seems to be obsessed with.*

***

Avery bounced directly from the awkward conversation into her office. She closed the door behind her, booted up her laptop, and looked down at the files on her desk. Sometime during her restless two hours of sleep, someone from the front office had delivered a file for Carolyn Rodgers to go along with the files for Sophie Lentz and Patty Dearborne.

Avery spread all of the material out on her desk. She then selected the pertinent info from each one and wrote it all out on her dry erase board. She rarely used the thing, but drastic times called for drastic measures. She listed out bullet points about each woman, along with the location of the body. She connected the dots as well as she could as her brain kicked into overdrive.

Petite women. Not much else in common—not backgrounds, not hair color, not eye color, nothing. No known links between the victims in terms of family or employers. No signs of sexual abuse. Clean skin, as if he was polishing them. He wants them to look their best, but he also wants their skin chilled, cold, almost blue.

"But why?" she said out loud.

She took some time to really pore over Carolyn Rodgers' file. She was thirty-six years old, the oldest of the victims. So age was another thing the victims didn't have in common. Still, Carolyn had looked pretty young, the sort of almost-forty woman that could have easily passed for thirty or maybe even twenty-five on a good day. She was vice president of the Boston Historical Society but she doubted that's what had attracted the killer. It was likely her modeling work, a few examples of which were inside the file. Carolyn had a sultry look to her, a set of bedroom eyes that seemed to burn off of the page.

If the ice is symbolic somehow, even if the killer doesn't know it, how would he view it? Why ice? Why the cold? If the killer has something against women, maybe he correlates the two—women and ice. Maybe something about frozen hearts? Or maybe...

An idea dawned on her then, one that had itched at her brain shortly after Patty Dearborne had been pulled from the Charles River. It was an idea that had clung loosely and then disappeared completely after that first letter had come in.

He's not only presenting them as frozen, but cleaned. Meticulously cared for. Is he freezing them to perhaps try to preserve them? Maybe he's trying to freeze beauty or something like that, trying to capture it as a form of art. And if that's the case...

"...then that's motive," she said, again speaking out loud. "It's nuts, but it would be a form of motive."

Okay, so if it's art, why the Charles River? Why the reservoir?

She felt that there could be potential clues now...if she approached the killer's mindset from this new skewed point of view. If she viewed the locations of the first two bodies as canvases in a way, there had to be an inspiration behind it. And now with Carolyn Rodgers displayed as a literal piece of art, it opened up other possibilities as well.

Still thinking, she gulped down the last of her mug of coffee and called up Ramirez. He answered on the first ring. "Hey," he said. "I was going to stop by your office, but the door was closed. And since you never close your door..."

95

"I know, I know," she said. "Are you here in the precinct now?"

"Yeah," he said. "Working with one of the profile guys to see what we can put together from this printout from the library. So far, it's not looking good."

"Look, could you do something for me? I need you to do some digging to see if there are any actual ice sculptor schools. Or maybe even just classes given at a community college or something. See if you can find that and a list of problem students. Anything weird or out of the ordinary."

"Yeah, I can do that," he said. "What are you up to?"

"I'm going to head back out to the Fresh Pond Reservoir," she said. "I might have a new lens to try to view this guy through. I'd also like to take a look at the scene in the light of day."

"Want some company?" he asked.

"I appreciate it, but no thanks. Not right now. I need to keep my head clear."

"You saying I dirty it up?" he asked with a sarcastic tone.

"Always. Call me with the sculpture school info when you have something and we'll meet up then."

"Sounds like a plan. Be careful out there."

"You know it," she said, and hung up.

She looked back to the dry erase board, taking it all in. When she felt she had a grasp on all of it, she headed out. Before marching outside and through the crowd of media swine for her car, she stopped for another cup of coffee. Not only was it bitterly cold out there, but she was going on only two hours of sleep and already, at 7:35, she had the feeling that this was going to be a very long day.

CHAPTER TWENTY THREE

The Fresh Pond Reservoir looked like a totally different place in the light of day. At night, it had looked gothic in some weird way; in the light of day, though, it looked both industrial and slightly forgotten. The morning sun shone dully down in the iced-over water, creating a series of sparkles that might have looked quite beautiful in any other situation.

Avery drove around its circumference, slowing down by the place where Sophie Lentz had been discovered. At once, Avery was pretty sure there was nothing remotely special about the place other than the fact that it had provided the killer with a fragile body of ice. For some reason or another, the killer had simply known about the place and assumed it would be mostly frozen. And because there were many more private frozen bodies of water in which to dispose of a body, it again made Avery certain that the killer wanted his little works of art to be easily found.

Near the backside of the reservoir, alongside a small building and a few attached pumps and other machinery that Avery didn't recognize, she saw a single vehicle. There were city tags on the windshield, indicating that it belonged there. Also, given the amount of ice on the windshield, it was apparent that the vehicle had been there for quite some time.

She turned around here and headed back toward the place where Sophie Lentz's body had been found. On the right side of the road, there was a thin dirt road marked off by posts and cables, blocking access. She parked and got out, looking to the other side of the road. A small grove of trees separated the road from the rather steep cement decline that led to the reservoir.

She walked to the grove of trees and looked out across the ice. It sparkled in the morning sun, throwing dull twinkles into the air. It was quiet out here, the silence broken only by the ambient hum of pumps and machinery somewhere nearby.

Is it always this quiet? The killer might have known this…in the same way he knew the ice sculpture park would be mostly dead when he hit it. Daughtry even said that to dump a body, you'd have to know your way around here. Looking at the lay of the land, I certainly buy into that.

Watching her footing, Avery started down the slight hill that held the grove of trees. Within several yards, she cleared the trees. A guardrail jutted out of the ground, the last line of defense between the trees and the reservoir. She climbed over this and looked out across the frozen water. It was seventy-five yards across, the ice a sheet of sparkling white between both sides.

As she looked to the left, back toward the way she had come from, she saw a man standing at the very lip of the concrete. He stood motionless, looking out across the ice. Avery thought nothing of it at first but then saw that he was wearing a dark coat. A dark puffy coat with a large hood.

She reached for her phone, ready to call in a suspicious character roughly a quarter of a mile away from a crime scene. But she wanted to be sure before making assumptions. The last thing she needed right now—with the mayor involved, the media in a frenzy, and the FBI sniffing the case out—was to make a wrong call. She sped up a bit, heading for the entrance of the grounds where there was a thin side road that wound back to the main highways.

She had no idea how the person had gotten down to the reservoir. There were no embankments that allowed cars on the sides of the road and a thin grove of trees between the right edge of the road and the icy reservoir. For the figure to have gotten down there meant that he had walked from somewhere nearby, as she had seen no other parked vehicles along the side of the road. This, she knew, was probably an indication that it was an employee who knew the grounds much better than she did.

She walked to the edge of the concrete and looked out across the ice. She was looking to the right, toward where she had stood a few days ago. She then scanned the area and when she peered to the left, she saw the figure again. Closer to him now, she could see that the figure was dressed in a black coat with the hood pulled up. The height made her think it was a man but it was impossible to tell. He was standing roughly twenty-five feet from her and had not noticed her yet. He seemed to be zoned out, looking across the ice deep in thought.

Avery started toward him slowly, walking along the concrete walkway that served as the lip of the reservoir. She had to watch her footing, as there was a considerable amount of ice on the cement. She nearly called out to him but if there *was* something off about him, she didn't want to alarm him.

As it turned out, she didn't have to worry about that. Within seconds, the man turned in her direction. The fluff of the hood triggered the memories in the security footage. She saw the low-turned mouth and sharp chin. This time, though, she could also see his eyes.

And those eyes looked alarmed.

More than alarmed, she thought. *He's afraid. Shocked, even...*

"One second, please," Avery said, still walking forward. "My name is Avery Bl—"

Before she could get her name out, the man turned and ran. He was incredibly fast, sprinting forward and then off of the lip and up through the thin grove of trees. It was evident that he had been here several times and had become familiar with the landscape. He was over the guardrail before Avery could even pick up her speed. She slanted back toward the flat expanse of land where the guardrail sat, hoping to cut him off. She reached for her sidearm at the same time, not wanting to fire a warning shot but fully prepared to do so if she needed to.

That's when her right foot stepped on a patch of ice right at the edge of the concrete. She was going too fast by then to catch her balance. Her right foot went flying out in front of her, followed by the left one. She was airborne for a moment and before she even had time to worry about where she would fall, she felt the very brief resistance of ice under her back and then the world went frigid as she splashed into the ice cold water of the reservoir.

It felt like knives at first—a million tiny knives slicing into her. Her breath seemed to freeze in her lungs but her muscles, on the other hand, were working overtime. She started swimming for the surface right away as the unimaginable chill of the water continued to stab at her.

She grasped the edge of the concrete and hauled herself out. She could barely feel her hands and it was hard to breathe at first. She looked toward the place where she had last seen the man but he was gone. Through the sound of her chattering teeth, Avery forced herself to her feet. She tried running but could manage only a stumble at first. It only took a few steps before she was able to sprint and then to run. All the while she trembled and shivered, feeling more embarrassed than anything else. But good God, the cold was indescribable.

As she started back through the grove of trees, she realized that she would likely not catch up to the figure. She heard a slight commotion up ahead in the woods somewhere but could not locate him. She tried her best to follow after the sound, which was made remarkably easy thanks to the cold ground and the freezing still morning. Actually, her own shivering noises and the clinking together of her teeth were the loudest noises.

She trudged through the trees and up the slight hill, wondering if her head had taken a harder impact than she thought. She was swimmy-headed and fighting to draw in breath. She was so

99

disoriented that she nearly ran into a tree. She stumbled and went to her knees. She got up right away and when she did, she could no longer hear the man moving through the forest.

Damn, she thought. *He's back on the main road. I have to get to him before he reaches his car—assuming he brought a vehicle.*

She fought past the cold, making fists of her hands and trying to keep her legs constantly in motion. As her body regenerated some of its warmth, she reached for her sidearm. She had it drawn just as she came out of the grove of trees but was unable to hold it steady through the shivering. She was standing in the ditch along the side of the road and although she looked to both sides, the figure was nowhere to be found.

She took a moment to weigh her options, fully aware of the importance of them. She could take a chance and continue pursuit on foot, not sure of which direction he had gone. Or she could go back to her car and drive up and down the road, hoping to see him.

He has *to have a car nearby. And if he reaches it while I'm on foot, there's no way I'll catch up to him.*

With this certainty in her head, she hurried back toward the car. She was finally able to draw in whole breaths and although the air itself was also cold, the shock of having fallen into the water seemed to be wearing off slowly. She ran back to the little cut-over spot where she had parked her car and cranked it to life right away. She fumbled with the heater controls, setting it to blast at full force.

When she pulled out onto the road, she started back toward the direction she thought the man had been running. Again, she was torn: did she drive slow to make sure not to miss him or speed ahead in the hopes of catching him if he was already making his escape further down the road?

After about a mile and a half further down the road, she again came to the end of the road where the small pump station sat. The two trucks she had seen there earlier remained but there was no third vehicle. She saw another small feeder road at the back end of this lot, mostly hidden by trees. Since she had not seen any other vehicles pass her by, she figured the man had to have escaped down this road.

She sped ahead, kicking up frozen gravel. When she reached the road, she pulled out her phone, thankful that the A1 had sprung for the expensive waterproof cases. Getting a little more control over her fingers, she opened up her GPS. She had no idea where this road led and wanted to have some sort of idea; if the man she was after knew them at all, he was likely far ahead of her by now. Barreling down the road, she saw the map on her phone's screen. A mile or so further ahead, there was a T-intersection. Either of those routes took her to more intersections, one of which would lead to a main thoroughfare that led back out toward Boston.

She raced toward the first intersection, pushing the car to seventy on the unfamiliar road. She figured there was no way the man had more than thirty seconds on her. Even if he knew the roads well, she still stood a chance of catching up to him.

She came to the T-intersection and took a moment to consider her next move. The GPS map showed that the right would lead her down a series of back roads that eventually dumped her out about three miles from the interstate. The left gave her a more direct route back toward Boston. And this killer seemed to have no locale of interest…so it was impossible to tell.

Shit, she thought, deciding to turn right in the hopes that the guy had taken back roads trying to outwit her.

She drove down the roads for the next fifteen minutes. She only passed two cars on the way, one of which was a state truck, probably headed to the pump station. The other was a small car being driven by an elderly woman who peered out over the steering wheel. By the time Avery started to see signs pointing her toward the interstate, she understood that she had lost him.

She sat at the stop sign at the final intersection for several seconds, letting her frustration have its moment. She was going to have to call Connelly and fill him in. And while there was no guarantee that the man she had chased was their killer, the coat was the same and he had run when she'd tried approaching him.

It was him, she thought. *This was our guy.*

She slammed her hand down on the steering wheel in anger. A jolt of dull pain raced up her arm, reminding her of her fall on the concrete and the reservoir. She headed toward the interstate and held her phone limply in her hand, wondering how in the hell she was supposed to explain this to Connelly and O'Malley.

CHAPTER TWENTY FOUR

She was on the interstate and heading back to the A1, listening to a heavy silence on the phone. She had just told Connelly about the incident on the iced-over reservoir. She remembered his humble sort of kindness earlier in the morning as he had dodged the mayor's request to lay into her. She wondered if that was the Connelly she was talking to in that moment.

"But there's no guarantee it was him?" Connelly asked.

"No. But the coat was an exact match. And if it was an employee or a state guy, he wouldn't have run."

She wasn't shivering quite as badly. The heater was doing its job but she was looking very forward to stopping by her house, jumping into a hot shower, and getting out of these freezing wet clothes.

"The look you got at his face…is it enough to recognize it from a lineup?"

"Maybe," she said, bringing the mostly concealed face to mind. "It would be a long shot."

"That's better than no shot," he said. "Are you okay?"

"Yeah," she said. She didn't want to admit how she felt like an absolute klutz from having fallen in the icy water. Her head was clear now and the almost paralyzing chill had left her, but she still felt slightly off. "Look, it might be a waste of resources, but if I send you the coordinates of the areas where he may have headed, maybe it's worth having a few guys out that way to canvass the area."

"Looking for what? A tall guy in a parka?"

"You're right," she said. "It's just—"

The phone beeped in her ear, indicating another call coming in. She checked the display and saw that it was Ramirez.

"Hey, I've got Ramirez beeping in," she told Connelly. "Let me grab this. It might be about a potential lead."

"Absolutely," Connelly said. "Anything to get this nightmare under wraps."

She ended the call and switched over to Ramirez. In the wake of what had just happened, it was good to hear his voice. "Please tell me you got something," she said.

"I do, actually. Something worth checking out at the very least. So, there's no actual ice sculpture schools in the state. In fact, from what I see, there's just three schools in the country that specialize in it. It's usually a technical college elective sort of thing. But I did find an instructor that taught an intensive course in ice sculpting a few times at a community college in town. I got him on the phone and he's waiting for us to swing by. So I figured you could pick me up at the precinct and we could ride over there together."

"You're amazing, Ramirez. Give me a while, though. I need to stop by the apartment."

"Why? What's up?"

She sighed and said, "I'll tell you later."

Avery ended the call, feeling wired and tired all at once. She looked to the clock and saw that it wasn't even 9:30 yet. *My God,* she thought. *This really is going to be a long day.*

***

The instructor's name was Gene Kirkpatrick and he worked out of a worn-down but quaint little studio in South End. After Avery buzzed in at the building's front door, Kirkpatrick let them in from his office. Avery and Ramirez took an old freight elevator up to his workspace. As it slowly ascended, Ramirez rolled his eyes and made a disgusted sound.

"Something wrong?" Avery asked.

"Artsy people," he said. "It figures that a guy that makes ice swans and angels would work in a studio with an old freight elevator."

"Feeling cramped?" she asked, trying to joke and keep things lively. Good God, she was tired. Having Ramirez with her helped a bit but not quite enough.

The elevator came to a stop and Ramirez slid the old wooden door open. It revealed a spacious studio, littered with old planks of wood, crates, several canvases, and two massive windows that let natural light pour in. Kirkpatrick was standing behind a small wooden desk, pouring himself a cup of coffee. He was wearing ratty jeans and a stained white T-shirt. His head was shaved but he had a thick beard that came down to his chest.

"Detectives," he said. "Good morning. I just brewed a fresh pot. Can I offer you some?"

"Please," Avery said, barely waiting a full second before giving her reply. She then managed to remain professional as they approached the desk. "Mr. Kirkpatrick, I'm Detective Avery Black and this is my partner, Detective Ramirez. We're here to ask about the classes you teach at the local community colleges."

"Yes, that's what Detective Ramirez was saying on the phone," Kirkpatrick said. "I'd be happy to help any way I could."

103

There were no chairs in the workspace, so when Avery accepted her cup of coffee from Kirkpatrick, she simply leaned against the desk and looked around. There were sketches on everything and the place was ripe with the smell of freshly sawed wood and paint. Apparently Kirkpatrick was about much more than just ice sculptures.

"First of all, I guess I should start out by asking how many classes you teach on an annual basis," Avery said.

"It varies," Kirkpatrick replied. "Most years I'll do two classes each semester. One of those four classes is always for ice sculpting."

"And are you currently teaching a class?" Avery asked.

"No, but I start another one in two weeks."

"How many students would you say you have in each of your classes?"

"I get a decent number for the woodworking classes. All of these HGTV shows have people thinking they can build damn near anything just like that," he said, with a snap of his fingers. "Every now and then I'll have a packed pottery class, too—about thirty students. As for the ice sculpting, those classes are usually pretty small. Eight to ten students."

"So would you say it's easy to remember the ice sculpting students?"

"Absolutely. Ice sculpting...I don't know. It takes a sort of elegance but also a brave mentality. Each little chisel mark you make is so important. No erasing, no kneading out your mistakes like with clay."

"And in the last few years, are there any students that stick out to you as being sort of erratic? Like a problem student or just someone you didn't feel comfortable around?"

Kirkpatrick chuckled and nodded his head. As he let out a sigh, Avery gulped from her coffee. It was quite strong, almost bitter, but it was exactly what she needed.

"Well, I've only been doing it for three years. But in those three years, I've only ever had a problem with one student...which is funny because he was only there for one class, technically. This was a guy that came in and was just...I don't know...*mad* at everything. Initially, he showed promise—real skill. But then out of nowhere, he went ballistic with the chisel and the hammer. He destroyed his practice sculpture. And when it was gone, he started yelling and attacking the work of others as well. I had to call campus security to have him removed. He came back to the next class but I wouldn't allow him in. See, the admissions department looked into his records and found that he had a criminal history that included sexual and aggravated assault. So security took him away. He never came back but he did send a nasty letter a few days later. It was in my little mailbox I shared with one of the painting instructors at the school."

"Was it a threatening letter?" Avery asked. *A letter,* she thought. *I wonder what sort of handwriting it was in. Would it match the two that have showed up at the precinct?*

"Sort of," Kirkpatrick said. "Mostly it just called me a talentless hack and that true art was chaos. Some shit like that."

Avery and Ramirez shared a look. *Art is chaos,* Avery thought. *A tired, clichéd-sounding statement, but also flatly poetic…just like our killer.*

"Do you happen to remember his name?" Avery asked.

"I do. And better than that, I can tell you where he works. The little bastard got really good at what he does and has been stealing business from me for a year and a half."

"Here in Boston?" Avery asked.

"Oh yeah. I'd be happy to point you in his direction."

Gotcha, Avery thought as Kirkpatrick wrote down the information on a scrap sheet of paper from his desk.

CHAPTER TWENTY FIVE

As it turned out, Kirkpatrick's information led them just six blocks further down the road. The section of South End really didn't change all that much. The only difference between Kirkpatrick's building and the building he sent them to was that it was sitting in the back of an alley that might have otherwise gone unnoticed.

Avery read the information on the sheet of paper Kirkpatrick had given them and tried to figure out why the name sounded so familiar. *Rustin George*, she thought. *I know I've heard that name before. But if he has a sexual and aggravated assault charge on his record, it would make sense that I've either read or heard his name in passing.*

While Ramirez parked at the back of the alley, directly in front of a door with a 233 over the door (per Kirkpatrick's directions), Avery wondered if it might be worth their time to call A1 and have someone from records pull up Rustin George's name. But that would only slow things down and for the first time during this case, she actually felt like they were making progress.

She shoved the idea aside and got out of the car with Ramirez. The back alley was eerily quiet and rather derelict for this part of town. She looked up at the single grimy window that sat several feet over the doorway marked 233 and saw that a light was on. According to Kirkpatrick, this was another studio space, more expensive than his own studio despite the condition of the place.

As they went to the door, Avery saw that there was no buzzer. She tried opening it and it came open easily. They stepped inside and she was surprised to see that the interior of the building was much nicer than the outside led her to believe. A set of stairs sat in front of them and an elevator was installed in the wall to the right. To the left was a large metal door with a sign reading NO ENTRY bolted into it.

"Stairs," Avery said. "I don't want the hum of the elevator to alert him to company."

With a nod from Ramirez, they started up the stairs. At the top, they came to a small landing. The wall in front of them boasted a large set of double doors. Through the glass along the center of the doors, Avery saw a studio on the other side—much larger than Kirkpatrick's but in a similar state of disarray. Loud music came from inside. Avery felt both nostalgic and, for just a moment, sort of cool when she recognized it as a Massive Attack song.

A doorbell sat to the right of the doors. Avery pushed it three times and then stepped back. Within a few seconds, the music came to a pause and footsteps started to approach the door. A man appeared from the right. He studied Avery and Ramirez through the glass, giving them a strange and perplexed look. He paused before answering the door. When he opened it, Avery felt a slight draft of cold air come wafting out.

"Can I help you?" the man asked.

"Yes, are you Rustin George?" Avery said.

"I am."

"I'm Avery Black with Boston's A1 Homicide Division. I was hoping you might have a few minutes to answer some questions."

"About what, exactly?"

From time to time, Avery had no qualms about lying to potential suspects. She liked to make them feel at ease, so long as she thought it might lead to answers. This happened to be one of those instances.

"Well, I don't know if you've seen the news lately, but we've recently been discovering bodies in frozen water—rivers, for example."

"Yes, I did see that," George said. There was a confused look on his face as he blocked their entrance into his studio.

"Well, we asked around about people that were into ice sculpting. Your name came up. You do ice sculptures for weddings and high-functioning parties, correct?"

"That's right."

"Well, we are leaning towards the theory that the man behind these murders sees what he does as a form of art. We'd like to speak with you to sort of get a glimpse into the mind of someone that works with ice."

"Oh," George said. His defenses slowly came down but Avery didn't think this automatically meant that he was innocent. He was eager to show what he knew, interested in helping them. That mentality aligned with the egomaniacal approach of their killer.

George stepped aside and let them in. Avery felt the cold chill again and this time it remained. She looked to the right and saw a metal door along the far wall just like the one they had seen downstairs. There was a series of tools on a small bench by the door—saws, chisels, and a few other odd-looking things.

"First of all," Avery said, "could you tell us where someone that wanted to learn about the art of ice might get started?"

"Other than online, there are a few classes here and there within community colleges," George said. "Sometimes you'll find

107

someone doing a free quote-unquote *class* at a public library or something, but those don't count."

"And where did you learn what you know?"

"I took a few classes here in Boston," he said. "But that didn't really get me what I needed, you know? So I went to this specialty class in New York for a few months. I learned a ton there. And then I came back here and opened up my business."

"And there's good money in it?" Ramirez asked.

"Absolutely," George said. "I mean, I have to do part-time stuff on the side to really make ends meet, but two or three sculptures a month make a big difference."

Avery pointed to the right side of the room, to the metal door. "And is that where you store your ice and your work?"

"It is," he said. "It's a modified walk-in freezer."

"And how cold does it stay in there?" Avery asked.

George now started to look suspicious. He walked over to the door the freezer and stood in front of it, just as he had done at the front door several moments ago. "I typically keep it at a flat twenty degrees. Sometimes I can go a little warmer, depending on the project."

A walk-in freezer to store bodies in, Avery speculated. *Plus a history of abuse and/or assault.* Suddenly, Rustin George was looking more and more like a probable suspect.

Before she could form her next question, George leaned against the door and shook his head as if he were disappointed. "We can cut the shit, okay?"

"Meaning what, exactly?" Avery asked.

"Well, there are bodies showing up in ice, yes? And I have a record that paints me as...what? A suspect?"

"Should we view you as a suspect?" Ramirez asked. He took two steps forward, making sure to place himself between Avery and George.

"Well, if you're asking me if I killed those women, the answer is no. But I'm not an idiot. I can see why you'd suspect someone like me."

"Can we look in your freezer?" Avery asked.

"I'm afraid not," George said. "I have a very fragile piece going right now and I have to let it set for a while. When you get into thin curves and detail, you have to let the cold really set in before you chisel away at the same point."

"You understand that your refusing to show us into the cooler is suspicious, right?" Avery asked.

"Not my problem," he said. "You lied to me so I'd let you into my office. So why should I cooperate?"

"Because it's a lot easier than making us get a search warrant and coming back here and getting what we want anyway," Avery said

George shrugged. "Do what you have to do, I guess."

"Come on, man," Ramirez said, stepping forward. "Don't make it harder than it has to be. You say you didn't kill those women, and I for one believe you. So help us out. Let's go ahead and eliminate you from the list of suspects."

Avery saw that George was reaching for the tool bench. She also saw all of the sharp tools on it. Before she could tell him to stop, George was speaking. And when he spoke this time, she knew that there was something unhinged about him.

"Each of these tools," he said, "is unique in its own way. They each break the ice differently. The guy you're looking for apparently appreciates ice. Anyone that uses it for art appreciates it. It's strong and delicate at the same time…"

His fingers danced over a chisel and then a tool that looked like a miniature scythe.

"Mr. George," she said. "Please step away from the workbench."

He ignored her completely, his fingers still sliding over the tools. He now had a faraway look in his eyes and his voice had gone monotone.

"I knew this day would come," he said and his voice sounded like he might be on the verge of tears. "When I beat that woman…I didn't mean to do the other thing…the thing that…God…her little girl…"

"Mr. George," Avery said, "I have no idea what you're talking about but we can figure it out." Slowly, she reached for her sidearm, the Glock suddenly calling to her.

"I didn't mean to," he said with a gasp.

In front of her, Ramirez had gone still. His hand was also hovering over his sidearm. Ahead of him, George was still grazing over his tools. He came to an old shop rag that was balled up in the center of the bench and stopped there.

"Mr. George, consider this your last warning," Avery said. "Step away from the bench."

He turned to look at them. Tears were running down his face. "So cold," he said. "It was so cold and I didn't know…I didn't know what I was doing and I'm sorry…"

With that, George tossed the dirty shop rag at them. Avery nearly pulled her gun, stopping herself when she realized that it was only a cloth. However, the weird form of attack *did* allow George enough of a distraction to open the freezer. By the time Ramirez lunged forward for George, the door was slammed shut.

"What the hell is he doing?" Ramirez asked.

"Pissing me off, for one thing," Avery said.

She walked to the freezer door and tried opening it only to find it locked from the inside. She hammered on it with her fist, feeling anger rising up in her.

"Mr. George, come out of there right now!"

When she stopped beating on the door, she could hear very light noises from inside. She also thought she heard something like the creaking of a door; it was very hard to tell due to the thickness of the freezer door.

"Is he trying to wait us out?" Ramirez said. "That doesn't seem very bright. It's got to be pretty cold in there, right?"

This is stupid, Avery thought. She knocked on the door two more times. "Mr. George, don't make this harder than it has to be. Come out here, please. We just need you to ask a few more questions."

There was absolute silence from inside. She shared a baffled look with Ramirez, not quite sure what to do. She supposed if George was truly trying to play a waiting game, she could call the A1 and have someone with special tools come out to take the door off. That, or she could—

The noise from behind her was so faint that she barely heard it. She turned around at the same moment Ramirez shoved her hard to the left and shouted: *"Down!"*

As she fell to her knees, she heard a gunshot. It was so unexpected that it was deafening. Following the sound of it, several things happened in the space of three seconds, making Avery feel dizzy.

First, Ramirez stumbled backward and fell to his knees. At that same moment, something warm and wet splashed against Avery's jacket and right hand. As she felt this, she saw Rustin George standing at the opened front door of his studio. He held a gun and there was a look of rage and fear on his face. She wondered how he could have possibly gotten behind them—and then she realized: there must have been a trap door somewhere in that freezer.

With the sound of George's gunshot ringing in her ears, she brought her own gun up and fired off two shots. She fired, pivoted, and fired again, taking George in both shoulders.

George stumbled back against the metal door, his gun dropping to the ground. At the same moment the gun clattered to the floor, Ramirez fell to his backside and then onto his back. Avery saw the blood at once, along his neck and soaking his shirt.

Her heart broke as she dashed away from him and toward George. She kicked George's gun away, quickly checked to make sure that neither of her shots had been fatal, and then went back to Ramirez. He was blinking his eyes as they wandered around aimlessly. He coughed and it sounded far too wet.

"Ramirez..." she said, trying her best not to lose control.

She placed her own gun on the floor and fumbled for her phone. With trembling hands, she put in the call.

"Officer and suspect down. Officer potentially in critical condition."

She looked back and forth from Rustin George to Ramirez. The place felt thick with approaching death and she could only hope it wasn't coming for the man that she was cradling in her arms as she sat on the floor in a growing pool of blood.

CHAPTER TWENTY SIX

Avery had remained with Ramirez for every second that passed between the moment she cradled him against her on the floor of Rustin George's studio to the moment he was wheeled through the double doors in the hospital, headed for surgery. She'd had no concept of time during the trip from the studio to the apartment. The very events that had occurred in the studio seemed hazy, as if she had been watching them from a faraway television screen.

However, hearing those double doors close and bend slightly in toward her snapped her out of it. She drew in a heavy shuddering breath and leaned back against the wall. A nurse rushed over to her and placed a reassuring hand on her shoulder.

"Are you okay?" the nurse asked.

Avery couldn't even get out a single word. She could only nod.

"Maybe you should visit the restroom," the nurse suggested. "You have blood on your clothes, your neck, and your hand."

Avery had known this—she had been very aware of it in the back of the ambulance as they had rushed Ramirez to the hospital— but it had somehow not occurred to her to wash it off. Again, she nodded weakly and stumbled off of the wall.

"Let me help you," the nurse said. "I'll grab some wash cloths."

Avery did not argue. In a dreamlike state, she let the nurse lead her into the restroom. With the nurse's help, Avery got the blood off of her neck, chin, and right hand. She watched it swirl in a pale red mess down the sink as the nurse rinsed the cloth out as she thought about what the other officers on the scene had told her. George had escaped into the freezer and taken a flight of stairs at the back of the freezer down to the first floor. He'd then circled back up to them and opened fire.

"Would you like me to take you to the waiting room?" the nurse asked.

The water on her face had brought her even further around. Avery was now getting a better grasp of things, the slight shock wearing off. "No, I think I'm good. Thank you for your help, though."

The nurse exited the restroom with her and they went their separate ways. "I'll have a nurse or doctor make sure to come out and notify you the moment there's any news," the nurse said as she left.

Avery gave another of her weak perfunctory nods and headed up the hallway to the waiting room. She could smell coffee brewing somewhere and knew that she'd need some if she planned to make it through the rest of the day. She glanced at her watch and was depressed to find that somehow it was not even noon yet.

At the waiting room, she saw Finley and O'Malley sitting in two chairs along the far wall. Finley got up right away and came over to her before she had a chance to take a seat. And God bless him, he had a cup of coffee in his hand, offering it out to her. She took it gratefully and wasted no time sipping it. It was bland and flavorless—telltale hospital brew—but she was happy to have it.

"How is he?" Finley asked as he returned to his seat.

Avery took the seat next to him and took another sip from the coffee. Finley and O'Malley waited anxiously for her to speak. She was surprised to find that it was hard to form the words to actually say it all out loud.

"They don't know yet," she said. "But the shot…it looked like it took him in the heart. It might have gone a little high but there was too much blood to tell for sure. The medics in the back of the ambulance didn't look optimistic."

Am I really saying these things right now? she wondered. *Is this really happening?*

It hurt to realize that it was…and this was not at all how she had expected such a trauma to go. She was worried and agonizing silently, yet not totally broken.

What does that say about me?

"Shit," O'Malley said. He voice was thin and for a moment, Avery could see the honest and caring man he was when not at work.

"Look," O'Malley went on, "the last thing I want you thinking about is work right now, but I figure I should at least key you in to what we found out about this Rustin George creep. He was arrested for aggravated sexual assault of an eighteen-year-old when he was twenty-three. A year and a half later he was arrested for domestic abuse and aggravated sexual assault on his wife. It was believed but never proven that he also beat the shit out of his wife's daughter— from another marriage, mind you. But the wife never came clean with the story even though doctors said the fractures to the eight-year-old girl's shoulder and wrist were clearly from having been beaten."

Vaguely, Avery could remember some of the nonsense George had been spewing before he escaped into the freezer. *"When I beat*

113

that woman...I didn't mean to do the other thing...the thing that...God...her little girl..."

"What was in the walk-in freezer?" Avery asked.

"Two ice sculptures in progress," O'Malley said. "But there was a downstairs to the thing. We found three pictures there...pictures of nude women. But from what we could tell from the pictures and the sculptures, he was just trying to recreate the pictures in the sculptures."

"We did look through his contacts on his phone," Finley said. "We found it odd that he had Carolyn Rodgers as a contact. We've got officers speaking with someone right now to see what the link is. Right now it looks like George did some sculptures for an event last year for the Historical Society and that's about it."

"Thanks," she said. She relaxed back in the chair and tried to ignore the fact that she was trembling.

"Listen," O'Malley said. "One of us can stay here with you if you want. But at least one of us needs to get back out there to grill the shit out of this guy. And if he turns out to not be the guy..."

He didn't finish the statement and that was fine with Avery. It was heavy on her mind, but for right now all she could think about was Ramirez. She was shocked to realize that in that moment, she honestly didn't give a damn about the case.

"I'm fine here by myself," she said. "You should both go. I don't need a babysitter."

"You sure?" Finley asked.

"Positive. Thanks for being here at all, though."

They both got to their feet and she could tell that Finley didn't feel right leaving her. With one last awkward look, he started to walk away. "Give me a call if you need anything," he said.

She watched them go and when they disappeared around the corner, she tilted her head back against the wall and allowed herself to cry. She kept replaying the scene over and over in her head, wondering what she could have done differently. Had she been too passive in asking George to stop moving? Should she have drawn her gun a little sooner, before he'd even had a chance to distract them with the cloth?

These and other questions swarmed in her head like hornets. She kept her eyes closed, telling herself that she was only resting her eyes. But if she happened to fall asleep for a quick power nap, that would be fine, too.

She opened her eyes when she heard footsteps coming toward her. A doctor was coming her way. Avery quickly glanced down at

114

her watch and saw that maybe she *had* dozed off for a few moments, as it was now 12:20.

"Detective Black...I'm Doctor Chambers, one of the surgeons that will be working on your partner. An initial check doesn't offer us much hope, I'm afraid. The fact that he's still alive is, quite frankly, a little baffling. The bullet did go all the way through, which is good. And it *barely* missed his heart, which is even better. But on its way out, I'm afraid it did some significant damage. Detective Ramirez has lost a lot of blood and his heart is pumping overtime due to the trauma, which makes it that much worse. He coded for about ten seconds but we got him back. We're working very hard to save him but please understand that we aren't out of the woods yet. And I'm afraid we won't know anything for certain for another hour or so and that's if he can make it through the surgery to repair the damage."

Avery nodded, taking the information in and processing it with her logical detective's brain. *Not out of the woods yet. Coded for ten seconds. Doesn't offer us much hope.*

Words like those did not make her feel very confident about Ramirez's chances. Still, she said nothing, remaining quiet as the doctor looked down at her sympathetically.

"I need to get back to it," Dr. Chambers said. "But please, let any of the nurses or workers at the guests' station know if you need anything. I'll do my very best to keep you updated as often as I can. Do you have any questions?"

She thought about several, but had none that she could adequately put words to. None that she was brave enough to ask, anyway. Dr. Chambers took his leave, hurrying out of the waiting room. No sooner had he left than a nurse entered the room. She had her hands tucked into the large pockets of her nurse's scrubs and something about it made her look like a nervous kid.

"Detective Black, I was one of the nurses that helped prep Detective Ramirez. As you know, his jacket and shirt were removed in the back of the ambulance. We just retrieved those items and...well, we found something else. I don't know what to do with it, exactly, but since you're the only one here with him, I thought I should give it to you."

"Of course," Avery said. "What is it?"

The nurse took her hands out of her pocket and extended her right hand to Avery. She saw the item clearly, but it made no sense to her; her brain was simply not able to make the connection.

Avery reached out and took it. "Thank you," she said.

The nurse gave a nod and left the waiting room, leaving Avery to look at the item that had been retrieved from Ramirez's coat.

It was a small black box. The exterior was soft to the touch, almost like velvet. When she opened it, the top opened on a hinge from the back of the box.

She stared at the engagement ring inside for quite some time, not even aware that she had started crying again.

CHAPTER TWENTY SEVEN

Avery was replying to texts from Finley while Ramirez was in surgery. It helped to distance her from the turmoil she was going through. Finley gave her constant updates concerning Rustin George while she also fielded texts from Rose, who was insisting that she come to the hospital to keep Avery company.

She was in mid-text with Rose when Dr. Chambers approached. She tried reading his face but it was quite difficult. She supposed being a doctor was another profession where you had to watch your expression at all times.

"The surgery went as well as it could," he said. "He's being taken to ICU. Give us five minutes to get him situated and you can see him."

"Thank you." She pocketed the phone and did her very best to bite back the tears that badly wanted to be spilled.

She waited until she was given the go-ahead and rushed directly to his room. In that moment, Finley and Rustin George may as well have been on another planet. Even thoughts of Rose went dim for a moment when she saw Ramirez. Seeing the state of him after surgery for the first time was the equivalent of a punch to the stomach. The man she had constantly seen as a source of strength and charisma pretty much since the first time she had met him was now lying in a hospital bed with several machines attached to him. He was unconscious and looked impossibly frail. As she took this in, the Dr. Chambers stood behind her, filling her in with his somber voice.

"The surgery was textbook and went well," Chambers said, stepping into the room behind her. "Our concern now is that he lost a lot of blood, but we managed to get him leveled back out. His chances of survival look better than they did two hours ago, but there's still no guarantees. The next few hours could be touch and go."

"Thanks," Avery said, her voice shallow. She walked to the chair by the bedside and sat down slowly. She wanted very badly to take her eyes away from Ramirez's current condition but could not. Her fingers reached into her jacket pocket and felt the shape of the ring box. Her heart ached at the feel of it.

How long has he had this? she wondered. *Was he planning to ask me today? Or has he been carrying it on him, waiting until the time was right? Is this why he shared that personal story about his first engagement?*

She reached out and took his hand.

"Let me know if you have any questions," Dr. Chambers said. "I'll be back now and then to check on him."

He left the room, closing the door behind him, leaving Avery alone with the mechanical hum of the machines that were currently keeping Ramirez alive.

***

Sometime later, she was nudged awake. Before even looking to the face of the person who had come into the room and stirred her awake (*but when the hell did I fall asleep?* she wondered), she checked her watch and saw that it was 3:12. She then looked up and saw Rose standing there. She looked timid and uncertain, obviously uncomfortable.

"Rose, what are you doing here?" she asked.

"Trying to be a good daughter." She looked over at Ramirez and frowned. "Is he going to be okay?"

"The doctors aren't making any guarantees just yet. But I think the fact he's made it this long is a good sign."

"God, Mom…were you with him when it happened?"

Avery nodded. "Right behind him."

"So…it could have been you? A few feet was all that separated you from being shot?"

Probably just a single foot, Avery thought but did not dare say it. "Rose, you didn't have to come here."

"I wanted to," she said. "I dig him, too…you know?"

"Thanks for coming, sweetie. I really do appreciate it."

"Did they get the guy that did it?"

Avery sat up and slowly started to tell Rose everything she knew about what had happened to Rustin George after she had shot him twice. She then backed up and told Rose about her morning. Speaking it all out loud actually seemed to ground her. It made it seem more real and it also made Ramirez seem almost heroic. When George had started to get sketchy, Ramirez had stepped forward…not just as her partner, but as her protector.

When she was done ten minutes later, Rose started to absently play with her mother's hair—kneading it and running it through her fingers in a comforting sort of gesture. Avery's heart warmed; it was probably the most emotional moment the two had shared since Rose had been eight or nine years old.

"Can I do anything for you?" Rose asked.

"No, you don't have to—"

118

"Shut it, Mom. What do you need?"

Avery chuckled. Her daughter sounded just like her. God, it was getting creepy. "I could use a bite to eat. And maybe a soda."

"I'm on it. Text me if you think of anything else."

Rose left the room, leaving Avery with the humming of the machines again. She estimated that she had dozed off for roughly an hour this time—long enough for her mouth to taste stale and her neck to go stiff. She saw two missed texts from Finley, keeping her up to date on matters with Rustin George. The first read: **He's been crying for the last twenty minutes. Confessed to beating the ex-wife's kid.** Another came twenty minutes later. **Connection to Carolyn Rodgers confirmed but not ill intent. Probably not our guy. Call me.**

She placed a call to Finley. Something about hearing the phone ring while also seeing Ramirez's motionless body in the hospital bed, all wires and a hospital gown, was surreal. Finley answered on the second ring. There was the noise of a slight commotion on the other end of the line.

"I just got your texts," Avery said. "So it looks like George isn't our guy?"

"I'm afraid not. He's a work, that's for sure. But it's looking like he's not the one we're looking for. Pretty sure you know this already, but it turns out he had ties to Carolyn Rodgers simply because he did some work for the historical society last spring. Also, he had an alibi for last night that checks out. Sorry, Avery."

"It's okay."

"How's Ramirez doing?" he asked.

"I'm not sure. The doctor seemed a little more hopeful when they moved him into ICU but they aren't saying he's in the clear just yet."

"And how are *you* doing?"

"I'm fine. Rose is here with me."

"Good," he said. "Again, you just let us know if there's anything we can do for you, okay?"

"I will, Finley. Thanks."

With the call over, Avery pulled out the engagement ring. She snapped open the box and looked at it. If she was being honest with herself, she wasn't sure what she would have said if he had asked her to marry him. She loved him…she was certain of that, even though neither one of them had said those words to the other yet. And she was beyond excited to have him living with her. But marriage…well, that was a different story altogether.

Then again, looking at him in that hospital bed and knowing he was there because he had, in a very real way, taken a bullet for her...well, that did something to her heart that she could not explain.

She held the ring in her hand for several minutes, looking back and forth from the diamond to Ramirez. When she heard the door opening behind her, Avery shoved the ring back into her pocket. That was a conversation she wasn't ready to have with Rose...not for a very long time. Hell, she wasn't sure she was even ready to have it with Ramirez. That was, of course, assuming she'd ever have the chance to have the conversation with him.

Rose handed her a Styrofoam container and a can of Coke. "Slim pickings down at the cafeteria," Rose said. "And I had to guess at what you'd like anyway."

Avery opened the container and was delighted to find a cheeseburger. It tasted like most hospital food tended to but she wolfed down half of it quickly. She hadn't eaten since breakfast and that had been just a very quick snack in the break room at the A1.

"Are you done with classes today?" Avery asked, doing what she could to keep her mind off of the reality in the bed in front of her.

"I've got one at six this afternoon," Rose said. "One of those lame courses I *have* to take. Business Communications. I think I'd rather be here—"

"No. Go to your class. There's really not much you can do, sweetie. I appreciate the company while you're here, though."

Rose pulled the second chair in the room—on the other side of Ramirez's bed—over beside Avery. They sat in silence as Avery finished her burger and sipped down the Coke. She appreciated the silence and was somehow sure that Rose knew this, too. And God bless her, she didn't just sit there and zone out in front of her phone. No...she was simply *there*.

And when Avery reached out and took her hand, Rose let her. More than that, she gave a reassuring squeeze.

***

When Rose left at 5:15 to make her 6:00 class, there was no change in Ramirez's status. Dr. Chambers had come by twice—once to let Avery know that he was leaving for the day but was leaving Ramirez in fully capable hands—and looked him over. Each time, he remained cautiously optimistic but would still not give any indication of an out-of-the-woods diagnosis.

As soon as Rose had left, Avery called Finley up again. When he did not answer, she tried O'Malley. He answered right away and sounded quite tired. Avery could sympathize.

"Any news on Ramirez?" O'Malley asked.

"The same. Recovering from surgery. Not out of the woods yet."

"Well, look…I appreciate your wanting to stay abreast on this case but we can handle it. If it's too much for you right now, we get it."

"No, I think I'd like to come back in on it. Could you maybe just give me until the morning?"

A silence passed over the line, a silence that she knew was filled with O'Malley thinking: *That gives this sadistic killer one more night to do his work.*

"Sure thing," O'Malley said. The tone in his voice was sorrowful but not cruel; still, Avery could hear the disappointment. If he had his way, she'd be back at the A1 right now, poring over every detail in each case file or out on the street chasing down their next lead.

"Thanks, O'Malley."

"Of course. I'll be praying that Ramirez pulls through. We all will."

With that, he ended the call. Avery slipped her phone into her jacket pocket, her fingers once again brushing the little box with the ring. She wanted to feel elated at the thought but instead felt…nothing. She was numb. The day had been too damned long and thrown too much at her. Slipping on the ice while chasing a man she assumed to be the killer seemed like it had happened a week ago.

She thought of that tall figure in the parka, the head drawn up and his head mostly covered. It was the last image in her head as she drifted off again, her exhausted body desperate for more than the scant four hours of rest it had received in the past thirty-six hours.

She saw the man again, standing by the edge of the frozen reservoir. But now he was not wearing the black parka. It was a cloak now, the end of which was fluttering in the frigid breeze. He turned and saw her and this time, he did not run. Instead, he came walking toward her—only *walking* wasn't exactly what he was doing. He seemed to be floating, coming along the concrete lip of the reservoir.

His face was fully revealed now. It was demonic, stretched into a smile that seemed far too wide for a human face.

121

"Why so cold, Avery?" he said. "Why are you always so cold?"

He chuckled and when the sound left his throat, the ice cracked beneath him. Avery tried to run but found that she couldn't. When she looked down, she saw that she was no longer standing on the concrete walkway, but on the ice. In fact, her feet were encased in it all the way up the ankles. She tried to scream but couldn't; like everything else, her voice was frozen.

As she was looking down to her feet, she saw a murky face underneath the glass. It was the face of the first victim, Patty Dearborne. She was screaming under there, beating at the ice, trying to break it to free herself. But the ice did not break, although Avery could feel it vibrating from Patty's weak fists.

"Sorry," Avery said, her voice literally freezing in the air and becoming frost.

One more punch from Patty cracked the ice. Cold water came gushing up along with Patty's arm. Instead of crawling out of the ice, though, she grabbed Avery's leg and pulled her down. The ice was like knives and the water beneath it somehow even worse than that.

Avery screamed. She flailed for help and the only thing her hands found to pull her out was a black cloak. She looked up as her body was slowly submerged in the water and saw that demonic face.

Avery let out a final scream and did not stop screaming until ice cold water ran into her mouth, choking her.

Avery sat up with a gasp, feeling as if she was really choking for a moment. She nearly fell out of the chair and it was that sense of falling that really snapped her out of it. *A dream,* she thought. *No, that was no dream. That was a nightmare.*

She got to her feet, surprised that she had managed to fall asleep yet again. This time when she checked her watch, she did a little double-take. It was 10:11. She had dozed in the chair for more than four hours. Her back was screaming agonies at her, but she felt surprisingly refreshed.

She went to the side of the bed and carefully sat down. The machines continued to hum by the bedside and Ramirez continued to be unaware of what was happening. She placed her hand in his and looked at his face. Had it not been for the tubes in his nose, she could have easily imagined that he was only sleeping. She leaned forward and kissed the corner of his mouth.

She knew that Rustin George had been cleared of the murders, but all the same, she felt that it was the killer that was still on the loose that was partly responsible for what had happened to Ramirez. She'd love nothing more than for him to wake up in this hospital bed and find out that she had captured that maniac that they had been after while he'd been shot. She didn't care if it was some sort of skewed justice; she felt that she needed to find this asshole now more than ever.

But she was stuck—just as stuck as she had been in the dream when the ice had her feet. With Rusting George cleared, there were again no leads. She supposed she could continue down the misunderstood artist route to hopefully find a few more, but she felt that they'd all be thin. She felt like she was missing something, some minute detail that might open up whole new avenues in this case.

Her mind took a dark turn as she came to this realization. There was a place she usually went when she felt stuck. It was a place that challenged her, a place that harbored a man that, whether she wanted to admit it or not, had remained some strange sort of constant in her life these last few years.

She gave Ramirez's hand a squeeze and made the decision.

Tomorrow morning, she'd go visit Howard Randall.

CHAPTER TWENTY EIGHT

After catching another few hours of uncomfortable sleep and the drone of late night television in the hospital, Avery gave Ramirez one more kiss, left a request at the nurses' station to contact her the moment there were any updates with her partner, and called a cab. She asked the driver to take her to her apartment where she showered, brushed her teeth, and changed clothes. The shower rejuvenated her and when she got behind the wheel of her car at 7:40 a.m., she started to get the usual jitters she experienced whenever she knew she was about to see Howard.

She arrived at the prison at 8:10 and had to bicker with the guards to let her see Howard so early. In the end they allowed it, bending to the name and reputation she had garnered during her visits over the last two years. They led her to the same basic room she'd been in numerous times before and when she sat down, she realized just how familiar it was to her.

I'm relying on him too much, she thought. *This has really got to stop—especially when I become sergeant.*

She reached into her pocket and grasped the ring box. She hoped Ramirez would forgive her for making this visit. He hated the fact that she sometimes came to Randall to get a better insight into the mind and motives of a killer. She understood it. It had to be psychologically unhealthy to keep coming back to him after the sordid past they had.

Desperate times and all that, Avery thought.

A few minutes later, the same door she had come in through opened up. Two guards escorted Howard through the door and to the opposite side of the table. Howard smiled at her, genuinely happy to see her.

"You good?" one of the guards asked her.

"Yeah, I'm good," she said. "Thanks."

They left her to Howard, leaving the room and locking the door. She knew they were standing guard outside, though.

"So good to see you," Howard said. "And so early in the morning! I assume you're here for a favor…seeing as how that's the only reason you seem to come by. I'm starting to think the Boston Police Department should owe me a stipend or something by this point."

"You have to believe me when I say that you are always a last resort," she said, her voice low and somber. God, he was good at making her feel low.

124

"I assume this is about the women that were discovered in the ice," Howard said. "The media is all over that one. And that poor woman that was made out to be a statue…"

When he trailed off, he let out a little laugh. It made her want to reach across the table and punch him in the face.

"My partner was shot yesterday," she said. "He was nearly killed. So if you don't mind, can you not be as sadistic as usual?"

He cut her an annoyed glance but it only lingered on his face for a few seconds. "Sorry to hear that," he said. "I heard about it on the news, of course. It was while in pursuit of this ice-killer, yes?"

"Yes. We were looking into an ice sculptor with a history of violence. Out of nowhere, he pulled a gun…not what we were expecting, obviously."

"Ah, but that's a mistake," he said. "However, before you churn my brilliant mind for some tidbit or other that I'm certain you hope will open up all sorts of possibilities, tell me about this partner."

"I don't think so," she spat.

"And why not? You come to me hoping for insights to capture your killer…and all I'm asking for is polite conversation. There's lots of talk in the place, but no stimulating conversation. So indulge me or get back to your clueless coworkers."

She nearly got up and walked away. *To hell with him,* she thought, gripping the edges of the table. But she remained seated, figuring she should make the best of the situation since she had already come out here and gone through the trouble.

"He's a good detective. He had good instincts and he's very good with hunting down information."

"And how are his people skills?"

"Basic," she said. "He's not the kind you'd send to talk to a grieving family, but he's also very relatable."

"Are you sleeping with him?"

She wanted to slap him. Yet, she also knew that the shock showing in her face had given him the answer. "Go to hell," she said.

"I ask only because you seemed very protective when I asked you to tell me about him. I just don't want human urges to interfere with your career, Detective Black."

"That's officially all you're getting out of me today," she said.

"Fair enough," Randall said. He looked across the room, thinking hard about something. Finally, he went on. "Now, I do think you are likely looking for a rejected artist of some kind. But I

125

doubt it would be an artist that has ever taken a class or really even thinks of himself as an artist."

"How do you mean?" Avery asked, hating how easy it was to follow along with him.

"Well, think of Hitler. He was a rejected artist, you know? Some say Manson was, too. He was something of a songwriter from what I hear. So I don't mean that this guy is an artist in the literal sense of the word. There are all sorts of artists out there—all sorts of people who consider themselves artists and their work as some sort of art. And I think this guy placing Carolyn Rodgers in a sculpture garden points to that. It's not so much about the creation of it as having someone see it...I think that's true of all artists. But when you get into the mindset of someone who deals in death and thinks of it as some sort of art, you have to break it down to an almost metaphysical level."

Howard Randall, talking about metaphysics, she thought. *Could there be anything anymore absurd?*

"Spiritual?" she said skeptically.

"Sort of," Howard said with a shrug.

"Well, you've read the letters, I'm sure," she said. "They're all over the news. Nothing in those speaks of someone with a spiritual drive to kill."

"Sure they do," he said. "Don't be so quick to dismiss someone as crazy."

"You're saying this guy is of a sound mind?"

Randall laughed heartily at this. "My dear, since the first man created the first weapon out of a bone or stick, no man has ever been of a sound mind. Not on this stinking planet. Tell me...was there anything of particular interest in those notes? Any alarms raised?"

"That they were almost like poems in the way they were arranged."

He smiled and nodded. "Excellent observation. That's correct. It's one of the first things I noticed as well. And if he takes such an approach with rubbing the police's nose in their ineptitude, then—"

"Then maybe every other part of his rituals is also poetic," Avery interrupted.

"That would be my guess," Howard said. "I think you are dealing with someone that is not killing for the sport of it or, quite frankly, even the *art* of it—though I think if you interrogated him, he'd claim art had something to do with it. No...there's something deeper there. The letters point to it, as does his use of ice and the cold. He's almost preserving them."

126

"He's focused on their beauty, but not in a sexual way."

Howard laughed again, louder this time. Avery cringed a bit. She was really growing to hate that sound. "See…you already have it all figured out. Although I'd throw in my sound mind argument here. I'd wager that just about any man with a violent streak also has some sort of sexual issue buried down deep."

"Perhaps," Avery considered.

"I'm not sure why you come here. Maybe it's not for help. You can do all of this on your own. I think maybe from time to time, you just start to miss me."

"Not quite," Avery said, getting to her feet. "You know, it's nice to see you're in a better mood these days. The last time we spoke, you were sort of a dick."

"Oh, I know. But things have changed since then. I'm involved in a little chess club we have going. There's a new guard on the block, too. He's a bookworm. We talk a lot."

"Good to see you're making new friends," Avery said. "On that note, I'll be going now."

"Glad I could help," Howard said with deep sarcasm. "Oh…and one last thing about your killer."

"What's that?"

"I think you're overlooking something that could be vital to a profile."

"Such as?"

He rolled his eyes playfully, as if annoyed but not really.

"Why winter? Why ice? For a man capable of these sorts of acts, I can guarantee you it's more than just some intangible symbolism with the cold."

"Care to elaborate?" Avery asked.

"No," he said with a snicker. "I can't do *all* of your work for you. What would be the fun of that?"

CHAPTER TWENTY NINE

He toyed with the idea of sending another letter. He had almost left one on the body he'd left in the sculpture garden but felt that it might flaw the presentation. He sat at his kitchen table, wondering what he might put in another letter. He grinned when he thought of it.

Police are not ice skaters. They do not understand the cold. A stumble on the ice and the rat has gotten away.

Or something like that.

The image of the woman who had come after him at the reservoir remained constant in his mind. And the fact that the woman had slipped proved to him that he was meant to do this work. Even nature was assisting him, the ice finally realizing his affection for it.

But he also knew that the policewoman finding him at the reservoir meant that they would capture him soon. And that was fine with him. When he'd started this, he wanted it to end in the custody of the police. He'd already gotten the media attention he had wanted. So when it came to an end, there would be cameras and reporters. And he could let it be known that he had finally learned how to cheat death—how to regain what had been lost.

Of course, there were still kinks in the process. With a few more tweaks and experiments, he thought he might be able to perfect it. It was partly about timing, but it was also about the strength and endurance of the body. To capture beauty, the cold and the ice did the trick. But to harness it…there was something more to it—something he had not yet learned to master.

He walked out of the kitchen and into the bathroom. He stared at himself in the mirror and studied himself. There was something very feminine to him, something he had learned to live with. Yet whenever he was drawn to these feminine qualities, it made him think of his mother. And when he thought of his mother, his heart felt like it had turned to ash and he became afraid of everything. He had learned to push her from his mind a long time ago but now, as he neared the end of his work, he had to face those ghosts.

He'd first been confused about his sexuality at the age of six. He was pretty sure that he was really a *she*. He could remember fleeting glimpses of the girl he had once been (the girl he still was, he supposed) and missed her. The long blonde hair, the bows in her hair, the girl-like smile.

128

But for reasons he had never understood, his mother had desperately wanted a boy. And anything he did that was girl-like was met with punishment and ridicule. He remembered his mother looking at him while he bathed, pointing to the area between his legs and telling him that God got it wrong—that she had asked for a boy…that the world *owed* her a boy.

It was the psychologists and policemen that made him realize that despite his mother's attempts at mind control, nature had had its say. He was a girl who had been raised as a boy by a mother with severe emotional and mental problems.

At such a young age, though, he had not realized her problems. When his mother had gone nuts when he had requested a doll for Christmas one year, he thought it was normal. When he pointed out pretty dresses in a store and was scolded for it, he thought that his mother just really didn't want him to have it. And when, on a cold winter night, his mother had pressed his face to the burner of a stove because he had finally summoned up the courage to tell her that he was a girl and he did not want to be a boy, he assumed it was a typical form of punishment.

He hadn't known any better.

He, he thought, looking at himself in the mirror. *He. Him. His.*

He ran his hand along the scars of that burn from long ago and shuddered. *But you're a she,* he thought. *She. Her. It's okay to accept that now.*

"No," he said with a croak.

Not only are you a woman, but you used to be so pretty.

It was a truth that hurt. When the first foster family had taken him in, they had let him live as a girl. They'd been okay that he had to pee sitting down. They bought him dresses. When he started to develop feelings for boys, they were okay with it.

So why am I still seeing myself as a he?

The questions were like hornets, always swarming in his (her) head.

When I'm beautiful again, that will fix it. When I steal their beauty and youth and freeze death…I can finally be free.

He lifted his shirt. There was no bra because he had never worn one, not even for the foster family that had raised him through his terrible teenage years. A few men had touched the breasts he saw in the mirror and it had been nice most of the time. But when he saw them, all he felt was shame. And, deep down, a longing to be able to accept them and the rest of his feminine form.

Almost, he thought. *Almost…*

129

He'd already decided that he would spend the rest of the day in search of his next subject. Two or three more…that's all it would take. He was sure of it.

He had some hard work ahead of him—work that never got easier. He did not like taking life but it always seemed to just sort of happen.

He went into the bedroom and looked out of the window. Everything was frozen and grim out there, crisp and almost featureless in the cold. It was beautiful in its own desolate way. It spoke to him. It called him.

He walked back into the kitchen and took the keys off of the peg by the front door.

The cold was calling him, and he had no real choice but to listen.

***

If he was being honest with himself, there was something he found a little sad about how easy it was to get his subjects. He supposed it was because women inherently felt safer around other women. And although he still saw himself as male, the women he preyed upon did not. They saw the long hair, the tall yet mostly feminine stature, and most of all, the scarring on the side of his face.

He was parked in the lower end of the parking lot of a local Whole Foods store, standing at the back of the van. The doors were open and he was doing his best to act—to play the part. He stood between two of the streetlights within the parking lot, slightly illuminated but not quite out in the open. The glare of the lights shone down on the fading darkness of the early morning hours. It was 6:22 in the morning. Not many people were out and about just yet, making it the perfect time. The store opened at 6:00 and while a few people had gone in and out of the store, he had not seen a woman that fit his standard; a few had been close but not quite perfect.

He was about to give up the hunt in this location and move elsewhere when he saw the woman quickly getting out of a little silver hybrid car up at the top of the parking lot. The first thing he noticed about her was that she was tall. The second thing he noticed was that even in the freezing cold, she looked to be wearing gym shorts of some kind that showed off a set of gorgeous legs. He glanced up and saw that the rest of her appeared to be just as promising through the somewhat tight-fitting T-shirt she was

130

wearing. He knew she was likely wearing a sports bra, too, so it was likely stifling some of what she truly looked like underneath.

When he realized that he had essentially marked his prey, a familiar surge of adrenaline and worry filled him. He felt dizzy for a moment, leaning against the van and working up his nerve. He wanted to take this one alive, and that meant playing the part of an actor. He had to convince the woman to trust him, to have no fear when he spoke to her.

He'd come up with a plan on his drive into the parking lot. It was simple, but he thought that was why it might work. And all it would take was a screwdriver and an old taillight bulb that had somehow ended up in his glove box several months ago. When he watched the woman who had just come from the gym walk into the store, he went to his glove box and retrieved the old bulb and the screwdriver. With them in hand, he went to the rear of the van again and did his best to appear busy. He angled himself so that he could see the front window of the store, his eyes on the registers so he could see when the woman came through.

Two cars entered the parking lot and three left in the time it took for the woman to appear in the window. She went to the self-checkout lane farthest to the right with just a few items in her hand. He waited until it appeared that she was slipping her credit card into the card reader and then started walking toward the store. He headed in the direction of the woman's hybrid car and found that he had timed it just right. He was nearly at her car as she came out of the automated doors.

At first, he pretended to not even notice her. But as their paths nearly crossed, he acted as if he had noticed her for the first time.

"Oh, hey, excuse me," he said, making sure that the feminine quality of his voice was at its softest. He also tossed a little embarrassment into his tone for good measure.

The woman looked up and within two seconds, she registered the scarring on his face and did her very best to hide her shock—not doing such a great job. It was clear that her shock was stopping the formation of words, so he spoke again before she had a chance.

"This is embarrassing, but a cop just pulled me over for a taillight being out. I told him I'd fix it right away. I knew the damn thing was out. I bought a new bulb three days ago and just never put it in. But...well..."

He then showed her the pinky on his left hand—the one he had dipped into dry ice for a little over ten minutes the day before. It wasn't quite as nasty-looking as it had been yesterday but it was still quite grisly.

131

Again, the woman did a terrible job of hiding her disgust. But there was a resigned sort of pity to her expression as well.

"Frostbite," he said. "I got it yesterday and I can't seem to pry the cover off the taillight. I can barely feel the finger at all. I hate to ask for such a dumb favor, but would you be at all willing to pop it off for me?"

The woman thought for a moment, and he could slowly see relief coming into her face. She looked to the screwdriver and the bulb in his hands and gave a brief smile. "Sure," she said.

"Oh my God, thank you so much," he said, leading her to his van.

When they reached the back of the van, he handed her the screwdriver. As she started to try prying the cover from the light, he peered back behind him and saw no one in the lot. There were only six cars and not a single person.

He reached into his coat pocket and withdrew the cloth with his homemade mixture on it. He could briefly smell it, strong and astringent, as he brought it out. He approached the woman from behind and placed it over her face.

But the woman was quick. Before he could clamp it down over her face, she had sensed something amiss. She stood up quickly and pushed the cloth away. At once her arms were working, one coming around and nearly clocking him in the face. He dropped the cloth, blocked the punch, and then felt instinct kick in. He punched her hard in the chest and, sensing that this was taking far too long, grabbed her by the chin and slammed the back of her head against the side of van in two successive motions.

The woman's eyes rolled into the back of her head and she slumped against the van. He caught her before she could hit the pavement and used his free hand to open the side door on the van.

He quickly slid her into the van, being careful not to let her head hit the floorboard as she angled her body between the middle row of seats and the back of the driver and passenger seats. As he closed the door on her, the sense of excitement died down and turned into something much more like anxiety. It broiled in his stomach like lava.

He turned his attention back to the parking lot. There was still no one out there, but someone was coming out of the automatic doors as he climbed into the driver's seat. He'd done it without anyone seeing him. Silently, he blessed the night for being so dark and the cold from keeping people out and about.

Having no idea how long the woman would be knocked out, he sped home, which was just five blocks away. He checked the

132

rearview mirror for anyone that might be following him or, God forbid, police lights. But all there was to see in the rearview mirror was his own reflection and just for a moment, he could almost appreciate and admire the woman he saw staring back at him.

***

He sat in the van outside of his townhouse for five minutes, waiting for a pair of teenagers that were hanging out on their porch three houses down to go inside. When they did, he wasted no time. Acting as quickly as he could, he removed the woman from the van. He did his very best to carry her as if she were just passed out drunk in case someone saw them, but it was very hard.

Even still, he was not all that worried about it. If he'd had the actual physical appearance of a man, it might draw tons of suspicion. But any witnesses would see two women stumbling up his stairs and inside, probably just a couple of girls that had gone out and had too many drinks.

He got into the front door without any visible prying eyes, closing and locking the door behind him. He set the woman carefully down on the couch. She groaned a bit and began to flex her fingers.

That's a good sign, he thought. *She'll be alive but maybe not totally conscious when I put her in.*

Sure, this was no frozen hamster…it was going to be a bit harder. But maybe, just maybe, it would work this time.

He picked her up and carried her threshold style to the stairway. His stairs split in two sections, one going upstairs and the other going down, the intersection meeting at the far end of his living room. He carefully carried her downstairs, the woman's limp weight heavier than he had imagined. By the time he reached the bottom of the stairs, his biceps were burning.

Still, he soldiered on. He opened up the room that had once been his office when he had worked at home as an editor. But the desk and computer were no longer there. The only thing occupying the room was an old storage freezer. He'd purchased it on Craigslist a year or so ago and had been working on it ever since then.

The adjoining bathroom was to the right and that's where he took the woman next. He set her down carefully in the bathtub and his arms were grateful for the relief. He then started to gently position her in ways that allowed him to easily take her clothes off. Being gym clothes, they came off rather easily. He put them in a neat pile on the floor. When she was completely naked, he studied

133

her for a moment. He'd have to shave her legs; they weren't bad, but the hair was noticeable. He also needed to do some work between her legs.

He had a small spray bottle on the sink filled with his chloroform mixture. He placed a single spray of it onto a washcloth and held it against the woman's nose for a few seconds. He watched her chest rise and fall as she breathed it in, knowing that such a small dose would be plenty to keep her immobile for at least another half an hour or so.

He then ran lukewarm water into the tub, filling it with roughly six inches of water. For the next fifteen minutes, he washed her and shaved her. He did so with deliberate care, working on her as if she were a valued family member that had fallen ill. When he was done, he dried her off and drained the tub. He patted her dry with a towel and then spread several towels out on the bathroom floor. He removed her from the tub and laid her out on the towels.

Looking at her, he saw that he had been right. She was gorgeous...even more so than the first woman he had used to start his work. He stared at her for a moment, spending the most time admiring her face.

Flawless...a thing of beauty.

Gathering his strength up again, he lifted her from the bathroom floor and walked back out into the study. He propped the woman's body up against the storage freezer and opened the lid. On the far end, where the woman's feet would go, was a vent where the liquid nitrogen would come streaming in. Another vent at the top, where he head would rest, circulated breathable air into the freezer so the subjects would not suffocate.

He looked at the ten-gallon tank of liquid nitrogen at the back end of the freezer. He had tried using it with the first two women and its effects had not had time to really take place before they died. He assumed they had passed because of the inhalation of far too much of his chloroform mixture. That or they had simply frozen to death and he, in his inexperience, had not been able to revive them.

But this woman...she was clearly still alive and he had been very sparing with the chloroform. As long as he kept a check on her (which was quite hard due to the inability to open the lid while the nitrogen was streaming in), she might be the one.

He checked his watch. It was 8:05. He set the alarm for seven hours ahead. He'd have to take her out by then. And even that was pushing it. It was a crapshoot, really. And if it didn't work with this woman, he'd have to try another...and another, and another until he got it to work.

134

He was smiling as he lifted the woman and painstakingly lowered her into the freezer. The lid stood three feet off of the carpet so it was quite hard to easily place her into the bottom but with great care and effort, he was able to do it. She was taller than the others so he had to bend her knees into little lesser-than symbols to fit her entire length inside.

He closed the lid slowly and softly, closing his eyes and relishing the sound it made as it closed. An opened Masterlock hung from a hinge that he had installed himself, one on the top of the lid and one on the body to keep it locked closed.

He then flipped on the air switch and waited for it to hum to life as air from within the room was circulated inside. That switch had been the hardest to create, as he'd had to hire a shady mechanic to do it for him. As for the valve for the liquid nitrogen, a few quick videos and studying a cryospa's mechanics had given him all he needed to know. Sure, it was still incredibly dangerous but he'd had no issues so far.

Lastly, he turned on the liquid nitrogen. It made a slight hissing noise as the nitrogen was distributed from the tank and into the freezer.

Before leaving, he snapped the lock closed. The sound of it clicking together was somehow magical to him.

He looked to the freezer for a very long time. With the other women, he had disposed of their bodies in ways he had seen as proper. The last one had gone into the sculpture park, mainly to taunt the police. To get attention. But mainly because she had been *so* beautiful; she had deserved a place among art.

He finally turned away from the freezer and headed upstairs. He was going to have to call in sick to work today, but that was fine with him. Eventually, he'd be found out and even when his work was proven—when he could actually capture beauty and harness it—he'd be seen as a monster. He knew that and understood it…but it would be worth it in the end.

As if promising this to himself, he ran his hand along the scar on his face and began to quietly cry.

CHAPTER THIRTY

Avery was studying the two letters that had come in while starting her morning with a proper cup of coffee. It was like drinking champagne compared to the gruel at the hospital. She did her best to focus, to put the trauma of the last twenty-four hours behind her. While her heart was still at the hospital with Ramirez, she also had a job to do. As she looked at the letters, rereading them over and over again for some sort of clue, a realization came to her.

The man I chased at the reservoir...it was definitely the killer. He wasn't expecting anyone to find him there. There has been no note to tease the cops or to boast about what he had done to Carolyn Rodgers. That's probably because my showing up at the reservoir threw him off of his game. And that could also mean he's going to act faster now—and that means the chances of him screwing up are much greater.

Or maybe using Carolyn was a letter of sorts in and of itself, she thought.

On the heels of that was the last comment Howard Randall had made: *For a man capable of these sorts of acts, I can guarantee you it's more than just some intangible symbolism with the cold...*

While she tried to decipher all of this, she called up Finley to see if she had missed any details and updates while she had blessedly gotten some rest. He seemed pleased to hear from her but she could also tell that he was verbally dancing around the topic of Ramirez.

"Well," Finley said, "the media is officially dubbing this guy the Ice Killer."

"That's pleasant," Avery said.

"Anyway... Rustin George is still in a holding cell. He'll be there for a while. He admitted some nasty stuff, bringing up crimes he had not been tried for in the past. If he's not our killer, he'll probably end up doing time one way or the other for what he did to Ramirez, of course."

"How about the picture we got from the library?" she asked.

"It's hit the papers but it's grainy and altogether useless. The moment it hit the papers, we got calls from the FBI. It's basically a waiting game right now; O'Malley expects the final call to come at any moment for them to take charge. He's down at City Hall, pulling some strings with the mayor to try to make sure that doesn't happen."

"Thanks, Finley."

She hung up before he had time to ask her how she was doing. She looked to the files and to her whiteboard, trying to tie up the loose ends with the vague theories she had started to piece together after speaking with Harold Randall.

When viewing the murders through the lens of someone that might be viewing the act of death and the presentation of the bodies more as a metaphysical act than a mere violent act of nature, it presented new options. It also presented new motives. Perhaps the man had an issue with the women that they had yet to uncover. Maybe he viewed the women as immoral....too much into their looks.

There were so many different ways to take it that it was overwhelming.

She again went to the whiteboard and jotted down new notes, looking to the pictures and assorted reports she had placed on the board with magnets. In all honesty, the notes she wrote down were not new. She had written them down several times in the last few days but with a new perspective, they *felt* new.

2 young girls. One mid-thirties.

Beauty. Perfection. No flaws (except tattoo, heavily scrubbed at).

Ice = frozen hearts? Frozen time? Purity?

She found herself drawing a line to connect *No flaws* and *Frozen time.*

Something about that seemed to click. She had wondered briefly two days ago if their killer was trying to preserve beauty. But if he was freezing these women because of their beauty and there was indeed some sort of metaphysical drive behind it all, maybe it wasn't the simple preservation of beauty he was after.

Maybe he's trying to capture *it,* she thought. *Maybe he's trying to freeze these women in the hopes of* taking *their beauty.*

It was eerie how easily she could buy into such psychotic theories. But to understand a killer, you had to learn to think like a killer. And just like that, another idea came to her. It was an idea so obvious that she wondered how she had not thought of it before.

Because it's borderline absurd, she told herself.

But she had no other options and in a strange way, this idea seemed to make sense. With the idea gaining traction in her head, she picked up her desk phone and punched in Finley's extension again He answered quickly with a simple "Yeah?"

"Finley, I've got a weird request for you."

"Good. The weirder the better."

137

"Can you get together any information A1 has on local cryogenics labs or research?"

"Cryo—what? Avery, are you kidding?"

"Nope."

"Isn't that just a bunch of sci-fi crap?"

"I don't know," she said. "I was hoping we could find out."

***

The search didn't take long because there was only one facility in the Boston metro area that fit the description she was looking for. Cryotherapy Partners and Solutions was located in the Back Bay area of town and while Avery was expecting something very much like Esben Technologies, she found something totally different. The place marketed itself as an upscale spa that, according to the website, "offered cutting edge cryotherapy solutions to prevent the telltale signs and pains that come with aging."

When she read the word *spa,* she nearly tuned out but then the tagline pulled her in. If her new hunch was correct and this guy was indeed trying to somehow capture and preserve beauty through the use of extremely cold temperatures, the chances were good that his interests were aligned with what Cryotherapy Partners and Solutions offered.

She called on the way over, setting up an appointment with the manager. Avery said nothing about being a detective, simply setting up an appointment to learn more about what the company did and how their practices worked. Based on that premise, the manager was more than happy to make the time.

After that call, she then placed a call to the hospital. After being bounced around from desk to desk, she was finally able to speak to a nurse about Ramirez. His condition had not changed, which, according to the nurse, could be seen as both a positive and a negative. Avery was then given the assurance that she would be the first person called at the slightest sign of a change one way or another.

She parked in front of the building, taking in its upscale design. It was the part of town where the rent for a place like this had to be astronomical. It made her assume that the prices for the services they provided were equally outrageous.

She walked inside and chatted quickly with a receptionist who looked like she had been torn right out of a *Maxim* magazine. After being told the manager would be right with her, Avery took a seat in the small waiting room. Soft jazz played over the speakers and

138

the lighting was so low that it felt more like a brooding coffee house than a cutting edge spa. She picked up a brochure from a small display against the wall and leafed through it.

All of the information inside of it had been taken from the website. It was quite vague, which made sense. She figured the science of it all would bore the casual reader. She did find the pictures within the brochure interesting. One of the three images showed a woman that looked as if she were made of plastic stepping into what looked like a futuristic tanning bed that had been tipped up on its front end so that it stood up vertically. The woman was wearing some sort of thick white garment that looked similar to the lead aprons x-ray techs often handed out before taking scans. A white mist was coming out of the machine and wrapping almost sensually around the woman's legs.

Avery's attention was drawn away from this odd-looking device when someone stepped into the room from behind the receptionist's area. She looked up and saw a woman that looked to be in her forties. She wore librarian-style glasses and her hair was up in a tight little bun. She looked almost annoyingly cheerful…what Rose would have called *spunky*.

"Are you Avery?" the woman asked.

"I am."

The woman extended her delicate hand to be shook and said: "I'm Leslie Deacon, the manager here at Cryotherapy Partners and Solutions. Come on back with me and we'll have a chat."

"Thank you," Avery said, setting down the brochure and following Leslie through the door by the receptionist's window. Leslie led her down a brightly lit hall where everything was white: the paint on the walls, the pictures in the hallway, even the carpet. They passed a few small offices before coming to a larger office. Leslie took a seat behind her desk and gestured for Avery to take the other one, sitting slightly to the side of the desk.

"Now," Leslie asked, "are you interested in cryotherapy for basic cosmetic reasons or is there an underlying illness or injury you are hoping to improve?"

"Neither, really," Avery said. "I suppose I should come clean, actually." With that, she removed her ID from her jacket pocket and showed it to Leslie. "I'm Avery Black, Homicide. I need to know everything I can about what you do here."

Leslie's eyes widened but it was out of shock more than anything else. It was the expression of a woman who had not been expecting police involvement in her business. *And that likely means she's not guilty,* Avery thought.

139

"Are we...in some sort of trouble?" Leslie asked. "I have to say, we've never faced any sort of legal issues before."

"No, nothing like that. I'm working a case where the suspect is rather obsessed with ice. His actions and mannerisms indicate that he has some sort of separation from reality, thinking that he can potentially freeze beauty and maybe even capture it for himself. I'd just like to get a better understanding of the work you do here in the hopes of getting a better understanding."

"My God," Leslie said. "That's terrible. Um...yes, I can tell you whatever you need to know."

And she would, too, Avery thought. Leslie looked scared and downright disgusted that the link had even been suggested.

"Just the basics will do," Avery said. "What is it you do here and how does it work?"

"Well, cryotherapy isn't really all that new but it *has* just recently started to get popular within certain circles. It started in Hollywood—one of those therapeutic things that was far too expensive and obscure for anyone but Hollywood folks. But it's getting more attention.

"Basically, cryotherapy involves submitting your body to extremely cold temperatures. Your body is essentially tricked into thinking that you're freezing to death. When that happens, your body kicks into survival mode. And when that happens, your blood is sent to all of your vital organs, sort of working overtime. This burns fat better than just about any other method there is. It's rather incredible. Then when the process is over, all of that oxygenated blood floods back to your extremities...and that is a very efficient way to rid the body of harmful toxins. So it's several benefits in one."

"And have these benefits been proven?" she asked.

"Several studies indicate as much, yes. But the US Food and Drug Administration haven't seen enough proof, so they always make a point to say that they have never seen any real evidence in their own studies and reports. As you might imagine, it's a rather controversial procedure."

"Have you undergone cryotherapy?" Avery asked.

"Several times, yes. It's worth noting that the anti-aging benefits are fairly obvious to see. Ask anyone that has undergone the treatment. It's an almost surefire way to boost metabolism, stimulate the production of collagen, and reduce all sorts of inflammation, most noticeably around the joints."

"And exactly how cold does it get in there?"

"We set our cryosauna to a negative two hundred and thirty degrees."

The number was staggering to Avery—so much so that she assumed Leslie was kidding at first. "I'm sorry," Avery said. "Did you say negative two hundred and thirty?"

"Yes."

"And how long is the person in the chamber for?"

"They are in the *cryosauna*—not a chamber, goodness no—for anywhere between two and a half and three minutes."

"And they come out fine?"

"Yes. There is a slight recovery process, of course. And there are a few safety precautions to take. We make sure each client is sweat-free. And if they are sweating before they step inside, we make them wait. We will encourage them to dry the sweat off with a towel."

"And what's wrong with sweat?" Avery asked.

"It gets cold enough in there to the point that a simple drop of sweat can cause frostbite."

My God, Avery thought. *The things people will do to look young...*

"And what do you use to get it so cold in there?"

"We use liquid nitrogen that is carefully regulated by a highly advanced system. It pours into the cryosauna until the desired temperature is reached. It is all controlled by the highly sensitive thermostat on the computer."

While Avery found this all fascinating and equally hard to fathom, she felt the conversation getting away from where she needed it to be. "What sort of requirements are necessary to work here?" she asked.

"It depends on the position, of course," Leslie said. "Most of us have therapeutic experience of some degree, with the exception of Anna, the receptionist."

"And how many people are cleared to actually run the cryosauna?"

"Well, there's myself and one other that oversee each session, but the controls are quite simple. It's all so automated that it's literally just the push of three buttons and the session is over."

"And what's the hiring process like?"

Leslie looked truly troubled for the first time since stepping into the waiting room about fifteen minutes ago. There was a flash of irritation in her eyes. "Forgive me," she said, "but is this a covert way of you asking if I think that anyone employed by Cryotherapy Partners and Solutions could be your killer?"

"Yes, that's the point I was getting to," Avery answered. "Given the information we have, it's at least worth looking into."

She'll object but give in, Avery thought. *She's too polite and too much of a professional to cause much of a fuss.*

"Well, that's ridiculous."

"Okay, let's take it down a notch," Avery said, wanting to keep things as civil as possible. "How about clients? Are there any that come in that you aren't quite certain of? Any that seem off?"

Leslie legitimately thought about it for a while and then shook her head. "None that I can think of."

"Okay. Then I'll make sure you ask the members of your staff when I speak with them," she said. She did not ask it...she *said* it. This was what she was going to do.

"Well, there are only seven of us. Five are here today. The sixth is on vacation in Maui. The seventh called in sick yesterday and is still not feeling well."

"How long has the sixth been in Maui?"

"A week. She comes back in two days."

"And what about this sick employee?"

For just a flickering moment, Avery caught an uneasy look on Leslie's face. It was clear that Leslie knew Avery had caught it because she looked down to the desk. "She's had some problems as of late. Behavioral sort of stuff. She was rude to the clients and complained of headaches. I'd like to fire her but...I just feel so bad for her."

Her, Avery thought. *Very likely not the killer.* "And why do you feel so bad for her?"

"It sounds shallow, I know...but she has a scar on her face—something she's had since birth. I thought it was important to have someone like her on staff so that the people that came in here didn't think I had an office full of Barbie dolls, you know? I think it's important to understand that sometimes life deals us a certain hand and that's okay."

You're right, that does sound shallow, Avery thought. *Hiring someone to fill some sort of quota just so everyone won't think you're discriminating. Classy.*

Avery thought all of this over and while there were no alarms sounding in her head, there *were* a few things that didn't quite sit right.

Behavior issues. Headaches. Sick for two days...

And she apparently has some sort of physical scarring. That might very will trigger some detached response toward trying to capture and harness beauty.

142

"I'd like the name and address of the sick employee, please," Avery said.

"I don't think that's necessary. It's also a violation of trust."

"Some might see it that way. You know who *won't*, though? The mayor. He wants this wrapped up as quickly as possible before he has a PR disaster on his hands. So if I call him and tell him you're holding up the investigation—"

"Fine, fine," Leslie said bitterly. "I can pull that up for you right now."

Good girl, Avery thought.

"Thank you. And in the meantime, I'd like to have a word with your other staff members as well."

"Help yourself," Leslie said, now not doing much to hide the fact that she was getting annoyed.

Avery left the office and did just that. She spoke to the other four employees that were there and found them helpful and, in most cases, eager to help her in any way they could. They all seemed to believe in the benefits of cryotherapy yet did not mind her questioning them about it. It seemed smooth and flawless until she spoke with the fifth employee—Anna, the receptionist.

When Avery asked her about the sick employee that often had headaches and had recently been rude and off-putting to some of the clients, Anna rolled her eyes.

"That's Erin. She's…well, she's interesting."

"And why do you say that?"

Anna bit at her lip and looked away for a moment. "I really don't want to gossip or talk bad about anyone."

"Even if it could help the police answer some questions?"

Anna sighed and gave a defeated shrug. "She looks at me in this really weird way sometimes. It's not like a *sexual* look but I feel like she's sizing me up for something. It's not the same as when you know a guy is sort of undressing you with your eyes, but it's close. Like a darker version of that."

Avery nodded and she started to get that familiar excitement in her gut—the excitement that came when she knew things were leading somewhere. She looked Anna over and had no problem at all seeing her as just as beautiful and flawless as the three women the killer had claimed so far. She had that same petite figure, the gorgeous face, the demeanor and glow that suggested that everything under her clothes was just as perfect.

"Did she ever actually physically bother you?" Avery asked.

"No. In fact, now that I think about it, it's almost as if she actively avoided it."

143

"And her scarring...does she ever draw attention to it?"

"Not on purpose," Anna said. "But sometimes I *have* seen her sort of running her fingers along it as a sort of habit. Right here, on the side of her face and along the bottom of her lip." Anna traced her own fingers along her face to show Avery.

It was then that Leslie entered the reception area. She had a sheet of paper with some very basic information on it.

"Erin DeVoss," Leslie said, handing Avery the paper. "I'd really appreciate it if you wouldn't let her know that I directed you to her. In all honestly I don't feel that I have. Erin has her issues, that's for sure. But she's no killer. The idea is ridiculous."

"I'm sure it is," Avery said, not so certain at all. "But I just have to check."

When she left the office, she could feel Leslie Deacon's eyes on her as she exited through the door. Avery didn't mind, though. It actually urged her on because although Leslie insisted that Erin DeVoss was not capable of being a killer, Avery knew worry when she saw it.

And in that last glance between them, Leslie Deacon's eyes had been filled with it.

CHAPTER THIRTY ONE

Avery parked her car in front of Erin DeVoss's house, directly behind a red van. She marked the van down on a mental checklist within her head. A van...perfect for transporting around bodies. She looked to the house for a minute and pulled out her phone. Her heart broke a bit when she instinctually pulled up Ramirez's number. With a lump in her throat, she instead went to Finley's number. He answered right away, either eager to please in the new role Connelly was inserting him into or legitimately worried about her.

"Look," she said. "I've got what might turn out to be a strong lead. I just wanted you to have the address in the event that I need assistance."

"Want me to come on over now? O'Malley would come with me, I think."

"No, not just yet. Let me get a gauge on the suspect first." She then gave Erin's name and address so that Finley would have it on hand if she needed backup for any reason.

With that done, she finally got out of the car. Before heading to Erin's house, she checked the van. It was a little ragged on the outside and it definitely seemed out of place in front of the townhouse Erin lived in. She was in the nice part of town, where Avery was pretty sure the rent for one of these townhomes was at least double the rent on her apartment. It was the sort of place people that bought into things like cryotherapy lived.

The van looked clean, although she did notice that the back seat had been folded down to allow for more space. She stepped away from the van and approached the front door. She knocked, still not quite sure how she was going to approach questioning Erin DeVoss. She'd have to be crafty while also playing into Erin's delusions.

Avery knocked a second time when the door was not answered. She had been standing on the porch for roughly one minute before she heard footfalls approaching from the other side of the door. When it was answered, it only opened about two inches, just enough for a single eye to peer out.

"Can I help you?" the woman on the other side said. Avery noticed at once that she was angled at the door so that the left side of her face was concealed.

"I think you just might," Avery said. "I'm Detective Avery Black and I'm looking into a very serious matter concerning the

145

people you work for. You do work for Cryotherapy Partners and Solutions, correct?"

Erin was quiet for a moment but Avery was having a hard time reading her expression. She seemed alarmed, sure, but Avery didn't see any fear in her face. "That's right," she finally said. "Is there something wrong?" she asked.

"That's what I'm trying to find out," Avery said. "Please...could you let me come in? I just have a few basic questions for you."

And there it was: fear. It flashed in Erin's eyes for a split second. As if sensing that she had given herself away, Erin stepped back and looked down at the floor. She pulled the door open and allowed Avery inside.

She took the place in at once, studying and observing. A very well-decorated living room sat to her left. It was well maintained and tidy, right down to the light blue carpet. To the left, there were stairs that led both upstairs and down.

But the sights were not what alarmed her. It was the *feel*. The place was absolutely frigid. She could hear electric heat humming in the house but she was pretty sure it had not been switched on until recently.

Erin led her into the living room like a good little hostess. Avery sat down on the end of a small couch while Erin remained standing

"Thank you," Avery said. "Leslie said you were sick. Are you doing better?"

"I think so," Erin said. "I think it was just one of those miserable head colds, you know?"

"Those are the worst," Avery said.

"So...what sort of trouble are we talking about?" Erin asked.

Straight to it...and very conversational. Also, if she was truly sick, why the hell is it so cold in here?

Undaunted, Avery continued, trying to act as if she wasn't cold beyond measure. "Well, there's been a very quiet report floating around about some cryospas using extreme temperatures. As I'm sure you know, that could be fatal. The NYPD has already busted a few places in New York for dropping the temperature about twenty degrees lower than the recommended two hundred and thirty. One client even went into shock and suffered brain damage."

"My goodness," Erin said. For the first time, she faced Avery head on. Avery saw the scarring on the side of her face. She'd seen worse in her line of work and was able to study it without staring.

146

"Anyway, we spoke with Leslie today and everything she said seems to be on the up and up," Avery said. "But when I discovered there was an employee out sick today, I had to take the chance. I figured I'd get a more honest answer out of an employee that wasn't surrounded by her co-workers at the time. Rest assured, Leslie has no idea that I'm here. So anything you might reveal, she won't know it came from you. You have my word."

"I see," Erin said.

In the midst of her explanation, Avery had seen relief show through where a flash of fear had resided only moments ago. That spelled guilt in most cases. Erin had been scared when she'd first realized she was being visited by a detective but then relieved when she'd discovered the bullshit reason.

Then she started to speak and when she did, her left hand went to the side of her face. Anna at the cryospa had mentioned this—a little nervous tic that Erin had. Avery watched her do it and took notice of the discolored pinky on her hand. She could not be certain by any means but it looked at first glance like it could very well be frostbite.

It's her, Avery thought. *But had the killer been a woman all along?*

She was feeling so certain that she nearly stopped paying attention to Erin as she answered Avery's fake question as well as she could. She caught the end of it, hearing enough to remain confident that Erin suspected nothing. She *did* appear to be nervous but her demeanor suggested that she was still relieved—almost like she was dodging a bullet.

"...and Leslie truly does have everyone's best interests at heart," Erin was saying. "She's a really professional lady and if there *is* anything underhanded doing on, anything *unsafe*, then I know nothing about it. It would really surprise me, though."

"Well, that's good to know," Avery said, getting to her feet. "Ms. DeVoss, I certainly thank you for your time. I'm all done here."

Erin got up quickly, clearly eager to show Avery back outside. Avery paused for a moment, not even looking in the direction of the door.

"Oh, there *is* one more thing," Avery said. She did not move an inch, standing her ground right there between Erin's foyer and the living room. Behind Erin, a small hallway led into the kitchen. Before the kitchen, a flight of stairs led both upstairs and downstairs.

"Yes?" Erin asked.

"Would you happen to know a woman by the name of Carolyn Rodgers?"

"I don't think so," Erin said, much too quickly for Avery's comfort.

"How about Patty Dearborne or Sophie Luntz?"

"I don't believe so," Erin said. Avery couldn't tell if she was being honest or not. For all Avery knew, Erin hadn't known the names of the women she had killed.

"And could you tell me what happened to the pinky on your left hand? It looks like frostbite."

The last word—*frostbite*—was what did it. Erin's eyes went wide but still, the fear was only fleeting. What Avery saw now was almost defiant.

You got me, those eyes seemed to say. *So what?*

Avery pulled her sidearm. She did not raise it to point it at Erin, but she made its presence known. "Erin...why don't you give me a little tour of your home?"

Erin said nothing at first. In fact, she seemed amused.

Clearly some sort of mental break...she's not thinking clearly. Or, rather, she is but her thoughts are clearly not logical or sane. This could be bad. I should have just told Finley to send backup right away.

"Don't you need a warrant?" Erin said.

"Probably," Avery said, pushing her worry aside. "But with the things I believe you've done, I'm pretty sure lack of a warrant will be swept under the rug when all is said and done. So save us the time and hassle, why don't you?"

Again, Erin was quiet for a few seconds before responding.

She's feeling me out...looking for a way out of this. Even though she had worked at trying to get caught, she wants a way out. Maybe she feels like her work isn't quite finished yet.

"There's nothing here," Erin finally said.

Avery realized that Erin's demeanor had not changed at all once the gun had been pulled. "You sure about that? Judging from the letters you sent the police and the media, it seems to me that you *wanted* to get caught."

Erin let out a huge sigh and then finally let her eyes take in the gun. She shook her head and smiled lazily. That smile was one of pride. She knew her game was up but rather than being upset, she was *proud* of what she had done.

"It's not that I wanted to get caught...not really," Erin said. "But I wanted people to know about what I was doing. I wanted

148

people to share in my knowledge—the knowledge that we can beat death. We can cheat it."

Gotcha, Avery thought. *Holy shit. Is she cocky or does she simply not care what happens?*

"Tell that to the three women I just mentioned," Avery said.

"You don't understand."

"I understand more than you think," Avery said. "Now move your ass."

Erin remained motionless, looking at the gun. With no choice left, Avery raised it and pointed it at her chest. She thought about the layout of the house, wondering where her best play would be.

Where would there be evidence? Kitchen? Bedroom? No...probably downstairs. It's out of sight and at the lowest part of the house...making for easy escape and clean-up.

"Downstairs," Avery said. *"Now."*

Slowly, Erin headed for the stairs. She was hesitant to turn her back on Avery but had to as she started to take the stairs down.

"I wasn't sure how long it would take the cops to figure it out," Erin said. "I was hoping it would get so far along that the FBI might get involved. The more attention my work gets, the better."

You were pretty damned close, Avery thought.

Erin reached the bottom of the stairs and turned to face Avery at once. Avery kept the gun trained on her as she stepped down. Ahead of them, a hallway led to a small walkway that led out onto a back porch. There was only one doorway along the hall ahead of them. Avery was pretty sure she heard something electrical running from behind the door.

"That room" Avery said, nodding toward the door.

"Well, I can't go in there right now," Erin said. "I'm in the middle of something."

The way she spoke made Avery fairly certain that Erin DeVoss was mentally unstable. Either she had absolutely no fear of the repercussions that would soon be coming down on her or she truly didn't think she was doing anything wrong.

Avery stepped closer to her, the gun still trained on her. "You do it or I will." She badly wanted to place her under arrest right there and then but so far she had not actually *seen* anything. She had the admission, sure. But this woman was clearly off her rocker, so her admission might not mean much.

With a little shrug, Erin walked toward the door. She turned the knob slowly, almost as if teasing Avery, and pushed it open. She walked inside slowly and Avery could see the cogs turning in Erin's head. She was trying to find a way out of this, a way to—

When Avery saw the large storage freezer against the far wall, she stopped. A tank of some sort was attached to one end of it. There was a humming noise as well as a very faint hissing.

"What's in there?" Avery said.

"Don't be stupid," Erin said. "You know."

Avery rushed to the freezer, strafing a bit to keep her Glock aimed at Erin. She tried opening the freezer with her free hand, so baffled by what she had stepped into that she didn't notice the lock for another several seconds.

"Where's the key?" she said.

"I don't think—"

"Get the key *now* or I'll figure out how to shut this thing off by myself."

Erin came forward with that same lackluster shrug. She reached into the front pocket of her jeans and pulled out a set of keys. As she passed Avery, she made a big display out of jingling them in front of her. "Fine," she said. "Happy?"

The keys jingling in front of her face caused just enough of a distraction. With the keys still dancing and making noise directly in her face. Avery didn't see the key coming at her face until it was too late.

Erin had the key trapped between her pointer and middle finger, using it as a sort of shiv as she sent a right-handed punch at Avery's face.

Avery brought her right hand up but not fast enough. The key hit her in the forehead. Not only did it gouge out a chunk of flesh, but it also hurt a hell of a lot more than Avery thought it would. It was like being struck in the head with a hard projectile and it sent her stumbling backward.

Erin came rushing at her and while Avery's first reaction was to fire off a shot, she resisted. If it went wild and struck the freezer, there was no telling what would happen. All she could do was regain her feet and fight back.

But as a thin river of blood from her forehead ran directly into her eye, fighting back was almost impossible. She sidestepped a charging attack from Erin but by the time she wheeled around to fire off a shot that would only hit the wall if she missed, Erin had launched herself into Avery's back in a thunderous shove.

Avery went flying into the front side of the freezer. When she struck it, something made a thudding noise inside. She could also hear Erin coming at her again but could not see her. The world had gone red and the headache that was spreading across her skull was like poison.

She waited until she could practically feel Erin's presence on her. She lifted the gun and fired twice. She heard a small, punctuated scream but then felt a huge right fist slam into the side of her head.

Avery managed to get back to her feet but as soon as she wiped the blood away from her face, she smelled something. It was strong and overpowering and—

Homemade chloroform, she thought, remembering the detail from the forensics reports.

As soon as this registered in her aching head, she felt a strong arm around her chest. When she tried to fight, she nearly got away but the chemicals spiraled into her brain and instead of fighting to her escape, she succumbed to the darkness.

It came quickly and like a soft inviting void that promised to take her away from the pain in her head, the blood in her eyes and the nearly fatally injured lover that she had left in the hopes of closing this case.

CHAPTER THIRTY TWO

Avery felt herself falling and then something hard hit her back. She tried opening her eyes at the pain in her back and along the back of her head, but they felt far too heavy. There was also something sticky on her face that seemed to keep her from opening her eyes. And with that sense of stickiness, it all came rushing back to her.

She finally pried her eyes open. She sat up and felt like she was drunk. She grabbed the open lid of the freezer and tried to pull herself up only to find that she was too weak.

Drugged, she thought. *Chloroform. Havre to fight it…stay with it…*

She peered out and saw Erin pulling a naked female body across the carpeted floor. She was headed for the bathroom. The young woman was a light shade of blue and motionless.

She was in here before me, Avery thought. *Erin took her out and put me in. I wonder if she's alive. I have to—*

In a dreamlike haze, she saw Erin set the woman down on the carpet and come rushing toward her.

"Oh, no no no," Erin said. She slapped Avery hard in the face, sending her back against the back wall of the freezer. Avery tried catching herself but she was far too wobbly. She looked up at Erin again, just in time to see something falling on top of her. It made no sense at first but when she heard a metallic clicking noise she figured out what was going on.

She was shut inside the freezer—this makeshift cryospa. Only Erin had no intention of making her look better or help get rid of signs of aging. She was going to freeze her to death. It was already cold inside, probably because it had been running only moments ago. That thought then led to another: she had been stripped of her clothes. She was stripped down to just her bra and panties. However, she was weirdly relieved to find that she had not been cleaned and shaved like the others.

That raised several questions, all of which paraded through her head in a panicked jumble.

That woman Erin was dragging across the floor was in here. Had she already been cleaned and shaved? Is she dead? Can she be saved?

What's about to happen to me? Can I get out?

152

Avery brought her legs up, hoping to get to her knees and push against the top of the freezer. She knew the lock would be holding the lid in place but she had to at least try.

At the same moment she realized that she was not going to be able to shift herself into the position to do this, she heard the sound of a small motor or engine kick on from somewhere very close by. A split second later, there was a hissing noise and the inside of the freezer grew immediately colder. It was pitch black, so she could see nothing—but she knew what it was. Whatever was in that tank was being pumped into the freezer.

Liquid nitrogen, she thought.

She took a series of deep breaths and tried clearing her head, trying to push away the effects of the chemicals she had breathed in. It had apparently been a small dose, maybe some that had been left over from the other woman and used in haste.

She thought of Ramirez, stuck in that hospital bed.

That can't be the last time I ever see him...

She bit back a cry of utter surprise and shock when she felt the freezer get unbearably cold. Her body started to shudder. She balled her hands into fists, trying to center herself, trying to keep her thoughts in order. There had to be some way out of this. But how...?

The freezer, she thought. *She made this herself. The tank and the piping I saw was not professional grade, and neither is the freezer itself. If I can inflict some damage on this thing...*

It was a long shot, but it was the only shot she had.

She drew her legs back again, drawing her knees up. She lashed out with a horizontal kick with as much power as she could muster. Her feet slammed into the back end of the freezer, the end where she had seen the tank hooked up. It stung her feet and every movement she made seemed to be hindered by an impossible cold—a cold she had never even dreamed existed.

Her teeth were chattering. She felt the coldness everywhere, so prevalent that it felt like it was literally seeping into her skin and filling every joint and muscle of her body. Still, she summoned up determination from the very pit of her heart and delivered another kick with both feet. And then another and another, seeing Ramirez in the hospital bed with each jolt.

The freezer trembled with each report. From outside of the freezer walls, she could barely hear Erin DeVoss's voice. She was yelling for Avery to stop it, to stop kicking at the inside of the freezer. Avery could hear it clearly now, the haze of the chemicals settling down to nearly nothing.

"Stop it right fucking NOW!" Erin was screaming.

Fat chance, Avery thought.

She drew back and kicked again, putting everything she had into it because she sensed her body may not be able to continue working in such a way as the liquid nitrogen continued to come pouring it.

With this last kick, the hissing noise stopped. There was a brief clattering noise and then silence. After a few seconds, she could hear Erin's voice again. She sounded very upset; fuming, in fact. There was a loud banging noise as she slapped at the top of the freezer.

Then Avery heard something that sent her heart soaring—a noise she had not expected to hear: the jingling of keys. She heard a commotion against the front side of the freezer. She could picture Erin slipping the key into the lock but could not imagine why.

While all of this happened, she could also hear Erin chanting something over and over, almost like a mantra. *"Oh you bitch, oh you bitch!"*

She stripped me to my underwear, Avery thought. *She has my gun. I broke her little human freezer. Maybe she's going to punish me. Maybe—*

There was a click as the lock was disengaged.

Willing herself to move despite the paralyzing cold, Avery drew her knees up one last time. Although she knew she didn't have enough room to get into a crouching position, she was pretty sure all she'd need was enough pressure on her feet to provide a nice push.

That and perfect timing.

Still shuddering and barely able to even *feel* her feet, much less use them, Avery pushed them down onto the floor of the freezer as well as she could. She brought her back up, pushing herself by the arms from the floor. She had to time it right or she was going to die. This thought went through her head like a bullet even as Erin opened the top of the freezer.

The moment Avery saw the light from that downstairs room where the lid had previously been, she sprang up as well as she could. Erin, clearly not expecting such a feat, didn't have time to move. Avery's blow was off but she still made an impact. Rather than delivering a hard uppercut directly under the chin, the punch went wide right. It clipped Erin's nose in a clumsy fashion, yet the effect was immediate.

Her hands went to her nose as blood flowed right away. She took a step backward in shock, allowing Avery to try climbing over

154

the side of the freezer. Her limbs were still shocked by the cold, though; rather than land gracefully on the floor, she landed in a heap of arms and legs and hair.

The cold had apparently stemmed the flow of blood from her head and without blood in her eyes, she could clearly see Erin come running at her. Avery noticed that she did not have the gun, which was likely her only saving grace. Erin lifted her leg and attempted to stomp down on Avery's back. She was able to roll out of the way, though, causing Erin to miss by about a foot.

With each motion outside of the freezer, Avery's body seemed to remember what it was for. As she got to her feet, she saw that one of the earlier shots she had gotten off had apparently struck Erin high in the right shoulder.

I've got to exploit that, Avery thought as Erin came rushing at her again.

Avery lashed out with her right hand, striking Erin directly in the gunshot wound in her shoulder.

Erin screamed and went to a knee in pain. And that was all the opportunity Avery needed.

She threw a knee up, striking Erin in the chin. Before she could rock backward to the floor, Avery wrapped an arm around her neck and tackled her to the floor. There, she applied a rear-naked choke, a move that proved easier to apply than she'd thought without clothes on.

Erin tried fighting out of it but each urgent movement in an attempt to get out of it only made her situation worse. The one time she did nearly get out of it, Avery moved her elbow down just enough to grate against the wound in her shoulder.

It took less than a minute before her struggles subsided and just another ten seconds or so before she was unconscious. Avery held on for another couple of seconds just to be safe. With a gasp of breath and shudders still passing through her, she let go. She rolled away and slowly got to her feet, bracing herself against the freezer.

With no idea of how long Erin DeVoss would be out, Avery stretched out her muscles, making sure they were in working order from the cold. When she felt confident, she looked around for her clothes.

She found them in the bathroom, alongside another pile of clothes. These were a woman's gym clothes—apparently belonging to the woman in the bathtub. When Avery checked her vitals, she discovered that the woman was ice cold. Avery detected a very weak pulse and wondered just how long this poor woman had been in the freezer.

She was in the freezer when Erin and I came down the stairs, she thought as she slipped into her pants. Feeling at least somewhat back to normal in regards to temperature, she grabbed her phone from her jacket and dialed up O'Malley.

"Yeah?" he said. "Any luck?"

Avery slipped her shirt over her head. She found her gun beneath the other woman's clothes and looked at it oddly, wondering why Erin had not simply killed her. Had she, Avery, also been meant to be a piece of Erin's art?

"Avery?" O'Malley said from the other end.

"Sorry," she said, snapping around and doing her very best not to dissolve into a mess of tears. "I'm here," she finally said. "I've got her."

"Got who!?" he asked.

She caught her breath.

"The killer."

CHAPTER THIRTY THREE

Avery found herself back in the hospital that afternoon, ironically, a floor beneath Ramirez. A nurse was putting six stitches in her forehead where Erin had assaulted her with the key. She'd been looked over for other injuries but had come out clean.

Finley was there with her, sitting in a chair against the wall and looking at pictures of items that had been taken out of Erin's trash can. "Hot off the presses," he said, showing her one of the pages.

"What is it?" Avery asked, wincing a bit as the nurse put in the final stitch.

"O'Malley and some of the other guys found rough drafts of each note Erin DeVoss sent out. They were crumpled up in the trash. One of them seems to have been written after Patty Dearborne was killed. In this rough draft, she actually even tells us her plans. Check this out: *How to capture beauty? How to repossess it...to take it from less worthy, those without scars, those that know no pain. And if I can't capture their beauty, I will dispose of them until it works. I will tame beauty and have death on its knees.*"

"Have they gotten anything out of her?" Avery asked.

"Nothing...just a bunch if crazy gibberish like this letter. She said she never meant to kill anyone...that the women we found in the ice were failed attempts at her work. She claims she sent the letters to us to get media attention. She thought her work would be misunderstood but appreciated one day. She wanted all eyes on it."

The nurse gave a little shudder as she finished up her work. "We're good here," she said. "Another doctor will come in soon to let you go."

Avery only nodded. She looked at Finley and asked: "How's the girl from Erin's house?"

"Not good. Her name is Melissa Carter and she was touch-and-go for the first hour after the paramedics had arrived. The doctors are fairly certain she'll make it but they *are* concerned about brain damage—but only time will tell."

"Thanks, Finley."

"Sure. Now, if you'll excuse me, I'm going to call Connelly and fill him in. You need anything?"

"No thanks. I'm good."

Finley left her alone and Avery found that she was literally jumping out of her skin to make it up to see Ramirez. She was fortunate that within five minutes a doctor came in, looked her over, and cleared her to leave.

Avery walked down the hall toward the elevator and saw Finley walking back toward her room.

"They letting you go?" he asked.

"Yeah. I'm heading up to see Ramirez. I'll catch up with you at work tomorrow."

"I'll pass it on," Finley said. "You know…with what you went through, you should maybe go see Sloane."

She knew he was just being kind and sweet in that clueless way he usually was, but something about the comment stung. He was probably right but with everything that was going on—with Ramirez and the sergeant position and patching things up with Rose—visiting a shrink on a regular basis was the last thing she needed.

"I'll think about it," she said. "And would you please keep me posted on the DeVoss case until I come in tomorrow?"

"Sure thing. Take care, Avery."

He gave her a brief and awkward hug before turning to leave. She appreciated it. He could have gotten on the elevator with her, waiting his turn to go down after she went up to see Ramirez. But he was giving her some space and she appreciated it.

Upstairs, she found Ramirez in the same condition she had left him in. She walked into the room slowly and walked toward his unresponsive body. She took his hand in hers and kissed it.

"So I got the killer," she said. "It was a woman. I'm sure you would have gotten some sort of morbid kick out of that."

She reached into her pocket and took out the ring box. The thought that it had been discarded with her clothes on the bathroom floor of Erin DeVoss's house sent a creeping chill through her.

"I won't lie," she said, tumbling it around with her fingers. "I don't know what I would say. But if you hurry the hell up and come back to me, we can talk about it. Sound good?"

She placed his hand back on the bed and took the same seat she had crashed in the previous night. While she still had a few hours before nightfall, she had no place else to go. She sat in the chair by Ramirez's bed and thought of becoming sergeant and, beyond that, what it might feel like to take a new position at work with an engagement ring on her hand.

A thin smile came to her face when she realized that one of those achievements was suddenly much more appealing than the other.

158

CHAPTER THIRTY FOUR

Avery was spoiling herself with a chai latte at Starbucks when she received the first of three terrible phone calls at 7:55 in the morning.

Her mind was elsewhere when the call came. She was thinking about how things had panned out with Erin DeVoss. A psychological evaluation had uncovered a number of issues, one of which could likely be used in court to get her off on an insanity charge. From what Avery knew, though, she'd still be confined to a psych ward and as far as Avery was concerned, that was a win.

In her interrogations, DeVoss had told about a traumatic childhood where her mother, starved for a son to spoil after her father had left, began to groom Erin as a boy, going so far as to change the spelling of her name to Aaron—more appropriate for a boy. The scarring on her face had come from a punishment for doing girl-oriented things; her mother had placed her face on a live stove burner. It was a tragic story, sure…but lots of killers had sad stories and as far as Avery was concerned, it was not her job to feel sympathy. It was her job to catch them to keep them from causing more harm.

And in that respect, Avery felt she had succeeded in the case of Erin DeVoss.

When her phone rang as she was collecting her coffee from the barista, Avery hoped it would be Dr. Chambers, letting her know that Ramirez had come around and was asking for her. When she saw it was Rose and then saw the early time, she started to worry right away.

"Rose?" she said, heading back out to her car with her latte in one hand and the phone in the other. "It's early. What's wrong?"

"I'm sorry to call you. It's so stupid."

"What is it, Rose?"

"It's Marcus. He…I don't think he meant to…but he hit me."

Fury flashed through Avery like a wind as she got behind the steering wheel of her car. "Is he still there?"

"Yeah."

Rose started to protest but Avery killed the call right away. She hit the road like a woman possessed. The stitches on her head were starting to itch and she knew this meant they were healing. They seemed to pulse slightly as she drove forward, reminding her that she was not invincible and that two days ago, she had been in a very precarious situation. Maybe she should slow down.

I'll slow down when I take that sergeant job, she thought, already resenting it. *Besides, personal life and work life are two different things.*

She blazed to Rose's apartment with no regard for the speed limit and came to a screeching halt on the other side of the apartment building. She wasted no time with the elevator when she reached the lobby. She went straight for the stairs. When her phone rang again she checked it just to see if it was Dr. Chambers. When she saw that it was Rose again, she ignored it and took the three flights of stairs up to Rose's apartment.

She knocked on the door and it was answered right away. Rose looked flustered and afraid. But there was also a red whelp on the side of her face.

Avery sneered and asked, "Is he still here?"

"Yes. I didn't tell him you were coming because I hoped you'd rethink things and—"

Avery walked into the little foyer and into the living room where she saw Marcus sitting on the couch. He had a laptop on his legs, watching a YouTube video.

He glanced up and apparently saw the look on Avery's face. He set the laptop aside and got to his feet.

"Mrs. Black, I didn't mean to. It was just an—"

Rather than punch him and cause some very serious damage, she gave him a hard open-handed slap across the face. He looked at her with shocked anger for a split second but it quickly dissolved into embarrassment and fear. She took a little too much pride in the fact that his bottom lip started to tremble.

"I dare you to try to tell me it was an accident," Avery said.

"Mom," Rose said, running into the room. But that was all she had to say when she saw the look of determination on her mother's face.

"Well, it wasn't on purpose," Marcus said, his lip still trembling. "I love Rose and would never hurt her. I don't...I don't know what I was thinking."

She punched him then and it felt far too good. The blow landed squarely on his nose and she heard it break. He roared in pain and stumbled backward. Before he could get too far away, she reached out and grabbed him by the back of the neck. She squeezed hard, pinching a nerve and driving him to his knees. He cried out in pain again but this one was muffled, as his hand was at his nose, catching the falling blood.

"What the hell?" he whined.

160

"Get out, Marcus," Avery said. "And if you think about reporting me for beating you up, just know that I have friends everywhere. Friends that you don't want on your bad side. Now...apologize to my daughter."

"I already did! I told her I was—"

"I said get out," Avery said.

"Go, Marcus," Rose said. "Go before she *really* kicks your ass."

Marcus got to his feet and did just that. He gave one final look back to both of them before taking his leave.

"Mom...you didn't have to," Rose said. "But I won't even pretend like I didn't enjoy watching that. It was sort of awesome."

"Rose, no man has the right to put his hands on you like that. You can't—"

Her phone rang again, interrupting her. When she checked it, she saw the number she had been looking for...one she had not programmed in but recognized right away. It was from the hospital.

"Hello?" she answered.

"Detective Black, this is Dr. Chambers. There have been some complications with your partner and we're going to have to rush him into surgery."

"What?" Avery said, sitting down hard on Rose's couch.

"He went into heart failure about twenty minutes ago. He's being prepped right now and I'll be scrubbing in. It's a risky surgery but without it, he won't last another hour. I just thought you'd want to know."

Avery was already halfway across the room before she said "Thanks" and killed the call.

"Mom? What is it?" Avery asked.

"Ramirez...he's—"

"Need me to come with you?"

Avery shook her head, struggling to keep the tears in, and left the apartment. The stairs were nothing more than blurs as she raced down them. She felt the tears sliding down her cheeks as she went through the lobby and then to her car.

Just as she got behind the wheel and clicked the safety belt into place, she got the third bad call of the morning. She answered the phone with trembling hands, not recognizing the number. She almost didn't answer it but thought it could maybe be someone from the hospital with an update.

"Hello?" she asked, doing her best to keep her voice from cracking.

"Yeah, is this Avery Black?" a man's voice asked.

161

"It is," she said.

"Detective Black, this is Nathan Everson from South Bay House of Corrections. We've um...well, there's a shit storm over here right now we thought you might like to know about."

"What is it?" she asked, her mind still on Ramirez and getting to him as quickly as she could.

"Well, it's Howard Randall."

"What about him?"

There was a heavy pause on the line before Everson responded.

"We have no clue how it happened," he said, "but Howard Randall has escaped."

NOW AVAILABLE!

A TRACE OF DEATH
(A Keri Locke Mystery--Book #1)

"A dynamic story line that grips from the first chapter and doesn't let go."
--Midwest Book Review, Diane Donovan (regarding Once Gone)

From #1 bestselling mystery author Blake Pierce comes a new masterpiece of psychological suspense.

Keri Locke, Missing Persons Detective in the Homicide division of the LAPD, remains haunted by the abduction of her own daughter, years before, never found. Still obsessed with finding her, Keri buries her grief the only way she knows how: by throwing herself into the cases of missing persons in Los Angeles.

A routine phone call from a worried mother of a high-schooler, only two hours missing, should be ignored. Yet something about the mother's voice strikes a chord, and Keri decides to investigate.

What she finds shocks her. The missing daughter—of a prominent senator—was hiding secrets no one knew. When all evidence points to a runaway, Keri is ordered off the case. And yet, despite pressure from her superiors, from the media, despite all trails going cold, the brilliant and obsessed Keri refuses to let it go. She knows she has but 48 hours if she has any chance of bringing this girl back alive.

A dark psychological thriller with heart-pounding suspense, A TRACE OF DEATH marks the debut of a riveting new series—and a beloved new character—that will leave you turning pages late into the night.

"A masterpiece of thriller and mystery! The author did a magnificent job developing characters with a psychological side that is so well described that we feel inside their minds, follow their fears and cheer for their success. The plot is very intelligent and will keep you entertained throughout the book. Full of twists, this book will keep you awake until the turn of the last page."

--Books and Movie Reviews, Roberto Mattos (re Once Gone)

Book #2 in the Keri Locke series is also now available!

Blake Pierce

Blake Pierce is author of the bestselling RILEY PAGE mystery series, which includes seven books (and counting). Blake Pierce is also the author of the MACKENZIE WHITE mystery series, comprising five books (and counting); of the AVERY BLACK mystery series, comprising four books; and of the new KERI LOCKE mystery series.

An avid reader and lifelong fan of the mystery and thriller genres, Blake loves to hear from you, so please feel free to visit www.blakepierceauthor.com to learn more and stay in touch.

BOOKS BY BLAKE PIERCE

RILEY PAIGE MYSTERY SERIES
ONCE GONE (Book #1)
ONCE TAKEN (Book #2)
ONCE CRAVED (Book #3)
ONCE LURED (Book #4)
ONCE HUNTED (Book #5)
ONCE PINED (Book #6)
ONCE FORSAKEN (Book #7)
ONCE COLD (Book #8)

MACKENZIE WHITE MYSTERY SERIES
BEFORE HE KILLS (Book #1)
BEFORE HE SEES (Book #2)
BEFORE HE COVETS (Book #3)
BEFORE HE TAKES (Book #4)
BEFORE HE NEEDS (Book #5)

AVERY BLACK MYSTERY SERIES
CAUSE TO KILL (Book #1)
CAUSE TO RUN (Book #2)
CAUSE TO HIDE (Book #3)
CAUSE TO FEAR (Book #4)

KERI LOCKE MYSTERY SERIES
A TRACE OF DEATH (Book #1)
A TRACE OF MURDER (Book #2)
A TRACE OF VICE (Book #3)

Made in the USA
Coppell, TX
26 March 2022

75578291R00100